# Girl in Shadows

# Girl in Shadows

Nymeria Publishing LLC

First published in the United States of America by
Nymeria Publishing LLC, 2021

Copyright © 2021 by Shannon Marzella



Nymeria Publishing
PO Box 85981
Lexington, SC 29073
Visit our website at www.nymeriapublishing.com

ISBN 978-1-7363027-1-2

Printed in U.S.A

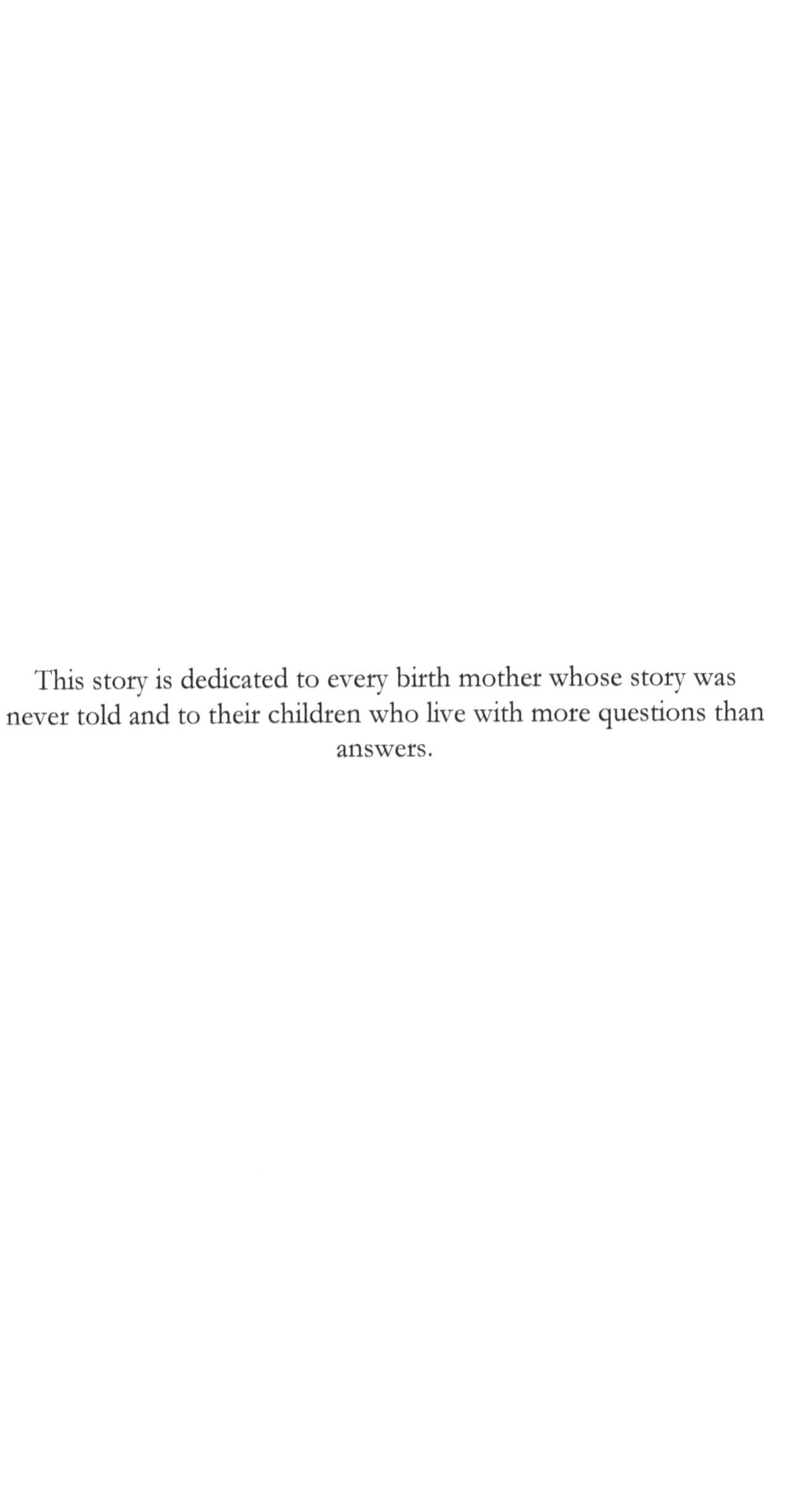

This story is dedicated to every birth mother whose story was never told and to their children who live with more questions than answers.

# January 3, 2001

The white plastic stick sat on the yellow Formica counter in the bathroom Nana was always too tired to clean.

Laura's fingers striped her vision, making the edge of the bathtub wobble in and out of form. The five minutes for test results ticked by, slow like cold maple syrup. Somewhere, possibly in another dimension, someone knocked insistently on the bathroom door.

A couple of hours earlier, Laura had slipped through the red double doors of her high school a little before the final bell rang and ran down the stairs to the sidewalk below.

*Avoid Sammy. No trip to the park today. Definitely stay clear of Joey. Make up a story later.*

The city bus whooshed to a stop in front of her, doors open wide like a mouth.

"Good afternoon, miss," said the bus driver.

"Afternoon," said Laura, head down. Change clinked.

*Payment to Charon on my way to the underworld.*

The bus crept along even slower than usual.

*Smells like spilled soda and sweat.*

The bright yellow sign of the pharmacy finally loomed ahead, and Laura rushed out the door, clutching her backpack. Her reflection stared back at her from the clear glass doors, but Laura couldn't meet her own eyes.

*Makeup aisle.*

*Medicine aisle.*

*Baby food.*

*There it is.*

Tucked into the back of the store, piled high with packages of pads and tampons, the aisle was a formidable foe. At the very end of the tunnel lurked the pregnancy tests.

*Deep breath, get ready. Please no one I know see me.*

Laura grabbed the cheapest test she could find and tucked it under her baggy sweater.

*Can I make a run for it?*

A security camera with a giant cyclops eye seemed to turn and look at her accusingly. Laura shivered.

*How humiliating would it be to get caught stealing a pregnancy test? They'd call Dad and Nana. The cops might get involved.*

Laura choked a little.

*What a way for Joey to find out.*

*No lines. Register close to the exit. That works.*

The clerk, about fifty with bleach blonde hair, snapped her gum and grabbed the test from Laura's hand.

*Just look at the gum, don't make eye contact.*

Colorful rows of gum, rainbow colors, neon colors, greeted her cheerfully. The clerk might have smirked a little bit while scanning the test, but Laura couldn't be sure. She was inspecting the gum too carefully.

*No matter. A smirk is far better than a look of concern. Silence is preferable, but a smirk's fine.*

"$12.32, sweetheart," the woman said with wide open jaws.

A pink glob of gum slid under the woman's tongue.

*$15, where is it?*

She had pulled the money from Nana's jar that morning before school.

*Here it is.*

The clerk handed Laura the change and the flimsy white bag, so annoyingly see-through. A few people slithered into the store. One of them looked familiar.

*Ugh.*

Metallic dread coated her mouth.

*Stay small, head down.*

Laura slid out, unnoticed.

Outside, Laura stuffed the bag into her backpack, punching it to the bottom. Nausea hit her stomach.

*Better not take the bus home.*

Instead, Laura began to walk the cracked side streets back to her house on the outskirts of the city.

Faded Christmas lights hung like drooping smiles from shop windows as she dodged quickly through the streets.

*Get home. Take the test before Maddy gets off the bus.*

Sometimes she caught a quick glimpse of her reflection in a window. Her body was lean and quick and her straight brown hair whipped behind her, caught like a windsock in the icy air.

The early January light was fading as Laura ran up the steps to her home. It wasn't a house, really. It was a duplex, and the family that lived on the other side of her walls were young and loud. They left toys, caked with months of mud, sitting on the small, unkempt lawn. At night, Laura could hear children's laughter and cries late into the night, much later than children should be up. The sounds were sometimes irritating but more often sadly comforting. It was somehow nice to know that people who were not her family were so close by. It made her feel safe in a very uncomfortable way.

Laura unlocked the front door and stepped inside. Drab brown carpeting that had collected dirt for decades greeted her as she took off her sneakers and put her backpack down on a bench. A faint smell of alcohol always lingered in the air, but it was not very strong at the moment.

*Dad's not home yet.*

The walls were covered with peeling yellow wallpaper. Laura couldn't help but notice them every time she stepped inside.

*So disgusting.*

Nana was sitting on a white couch with an afternoon talk show blaring loudly from the television. The gentle sound of snoring emanated from her mouth, somehow audible above the wide-mouthed faces jabbering on the screen.

*One less obstacle to the bathroom.*

The bathroom door was locked, Laura made sure of it. Pulling the pharmacy bag out of her backpack, the pregnancy test packaging looked happy and pink. She took a gulp of air and held her breath.

*Damn the crinkly packaging, why must it be so loud?*

The pregnancy test looked so simple, so clean. Her jeans and underwear left red streaks on her thighs as she yanked them down, her heart pounding in her thin chest. While urinating for  the five seconds, the cold sensation of dread seeped through her bones. The anticipation, the fear, the questions had all loomed over her for the past few weeks since her missed period. The thought of a baby had never actually felt real. Laura had worried about her dad's reaction, school, her friends, and Maddy. About Joey and Sammy. Especially about Joey. The baby was an afterthought, a possibility so vast and incomprehensible that it had not even seemed like part of the story until this very moment, as she watched the pale urine stream from between her legs.

She laid the test down carefully on the bathroom sink according to the instruction pamphlet. Her body was hollow and empty. It was hard to imagine that her own heart was still there, beating inside of her, let alone a second life living deep in her belly.

The sound of knocking stirred her from the blank reservoir of her mind. Maddy.

"I'll be right out," Laura called.

 "I have to go!" Maddy said insistently.

"Just give me a minute,"

"No, I can't," Maddy cried, whining as if she were three rather than ten.

"Okay, okay."

At least five minutes must have passed. Laura looked over at the test. *Another monster to face.*

Her vision swam as she crossed the vast expanse of time and space. What she saw was both completely unsurprising and world shattering. The cross was there and the memory of kneeling at the altar in church flashed in front of her eyes. Laura placed a damp hand on the yellow Formica counter, lifted the toilet seat, and vomited into the brown bowl.

# July 1999

Laura had spent the afternoon huddled under a large ash tree at the park. *A Tree Grows in Brooklyn* lay beside her, untouched. The hot day had left her drenched in sweat, but as she pressed the back of her head against the tree's cool trunk, the heat began to pour out of her body. Laura had always loved the quiet of old trees. In elementary school, she had climbed them as high up as possible. Most of her friends were afraid of heights. Laura loved the freedom. Her feet would reach for each open branch easily, as she found herself higher and higher above the earth. Up there her breath flowed with ease. Her rib cage would relax enough to allow deep, full breaths to penetrate her lungs. The air almost had a taste, like flowers and grass.

Sitting beneath the tree, she could hear the far-off sounds of children playing. Closing her eyes, she listened to the Earth.

*"Listen," her mother said. "You can't feel the Earth spinning, but sometimes, I think, I can hear it. Do you?"*

*She wore a mischievous smile like they were sharing a secret.*

*Laura bent her scraped knees onto the ground and pressed her palms, stained with marker and ink, on the deep earth. A gentle hum arose in her mind.*

*"Yes, I hear it!" she cried, excitedly.*

*Her mother smiled and they passed the next hour laying on the earth in silence, listening.*

*When she arrived at school the next morning and proudly announced her discovery to the teacher and the rest of the class, her words were met with laughter. The teacher's laughter was good natured, but the children's laughter bordered on cruel. Amidst the laughter, she stated quietly, yet loudly enough for everyone to hear, "Just because you don't hear it doesn't mean that it's not there." The words were spoken without malice or arrogance, but they silenced the class, including the teacher, who quickly redirected the students back to chapter four.*

Her mother was like earth, an anchor to everything rooted and safe. The weeks since her death were like floating through outer space, directionless. Laura had been the one who found her. The memory of it was etched into her brain, and nightmares of that moment visited her almost nightly.

*The alarm for school had gone off as it always did, but the house didn't smell like coffee. That was the first clue that something was wrong.*

*Laura had called through the house, "Mom?"*

*Opening her sister's bedroom door quietly, Laura saw that Maddy was still fast asleep, her cheeks soft and dimpled.*

*Shouldn't wake her yet.*

*Laura had closed the door softly behind her.*

*The light in the house was soft grey and out of the kitchen window pink fog embraced the rising sun. Laura had dragged her hand along the white walls, beneath the school pictures and family portraits her mother's hands had carefully framed and hung.*

*"Mom!" Laura had called again.*

*Why isn't she up yet?*

*Her stomach rumbled. Normally, a nice plate of scrambled eggs and a glass of orange juice were waiting for her. Her mother's bedroom door was shut tight. Laura had opened it carefully and peeked in. She saw her mother draped like a swan across the bed. There was a strange stillness in the room. The long, pale body was covered as if in swaddling clothes by a white duvet and soft pillows. One of her mother's arms was hanging over the edge of the bed slightly, in an odd way.*

*Laura couldn't see her face, so she called again, "Mom?" this time in a softer tone, questioning, yearning.*

*There was no answer. Creeping forward, she could see half of her mother's face. It was white and expressionless. Laura leapt forward and began to shake her mother. She shook her hard, and it sounded like someone was screaming and crying, but she wasn't sure who.*

*Mom held me in place.*

Now, mornings were cold and dark, her father at work, no one to perform the simple, mundane tasks so easy to take for granted.

*Dad, also spiraling out in his own way. More bottles, more mess, more yelling.*

The funeral was just a couple of months ago, but it could have just as well been many years ago or just a few minutes. The day had been rainy, but it also felt impossibly hot and sticky, a conundrum of weather that made Laura want to peel off her wet skin like a soggy raincoat. Laura had woken early the morning of the funeral to the sounds of spring birds chirping. The light in her room was black with just a hint of gray as the world spun closer to the brightness of the summer solstice. Laura did not feel bright. In the few days since her mother's death, there had been a heavy emptiness in the house, as if she were carrying invisible bricks everywhere.

She and Maddy had been pulled from school, and the phone had been ringing constantly with offers of condolences. Word had spread through the town. Laura dreaded the day she would have to step back into school, forever labeled the kid whose mom died. In fifth grade, Lawrence Sachs was diagnosed with Leukemia. There were pictures of him without hair posted at fundraisers, rallies to help the family with the funds they needed to save him from his own war-torn body. It was ironic, the naked vulnerability of asking for money and having her picture posted all around town without hair in exchange for survival. Privacy was a privilege and one that she wouldn't know again for a long time, if ever. Her private horror would be cataloged in the collective memory of her town so that, even decades from now, she would be remembered by former classmates as the girl whose mom died in eighth grade.

Later, there was a blur of hot shower water and black clothes as she prepared for the funeral. Maddy would sometimes perforate the numb bubble Laura found herself moving in. She would appear, like a small ghost with red, swollen eyes, asking for help with her stockings or needing someone to brush her hair. Laura performed these tasks mechanically, cognizant somewhere in the recesses of her mind that she would now be responsible for the many things her mother used to do to care for Maddy.

They arrived at the funeral home at ten o'clock. Laura walked up the concrete steps, her stomach swimming. Behind her, Nana and Maddy held hands. The room smelled of sickly sweet carnations and flowers in bloom. Her mother lay stiffly in a coffin with a white, pillowy dress on.

*Why did they put her in that dress? I love that dress, and now it's going to be buried in the dirt with her forever.*

The gauzy softness of the white dress, the feel of it, belonged to Laura and no one else. Her mother would wear it on warm summer days when they would spend afternoons in the backyard, collecting flowers, watching white clouds pass. Sometimes, she would lay her head down on her mother's lap and enjoy the soft stroking sensations on her scalp as her mother played with her hair.

Cut flowers, dead flowers, were positioned on and around her, flowers that were forced to bloom in an artificial environment surrounding a body with no life, animated by makeup and chemicals. Someone had drawn red lipstick on her mother's mouth and pulled back her long, straight blonde hair. Pearl earrings were fastened to her earlobes and a small silver cross hung around her neck.

*Maybe with that cross on, she'll be able to sneak into heaven.*

Laura laughed joylessly at this quiet thought.

After the funeral home, they had driven to the church in silence. Inside the church, Laura had slipped into the front row, next to Nana and Maddy. Her father sat just behind them. The wooden box containing her mother paraded down the aisle. Laura looked down, unable to watch. Instead of feeling herself squarely in the pew, she found herself floating up and out of her body, to the highest height of the cathedral ceiling in the church.

*Look at those little heads, bobbing in a row to Ave Maria. And the priest, his bald head looks like a shiny ornament. And Mom's coffin looks like a Monopoly house. Maybe it's because I'm floating up here, but upside-down Jesus looks like a bat.*

Reversed, Jesus' smile turned into a frown, and his wings wanted to swallow her whole. Laura imagined looking into his clear brown eyes and asking for forgiveness for her sins, as she had been taught to do in her religion classes that Nana made her attend. Being raised loosely Irish Catholic, guilt and the need for repentance had seeped into her DNA, or so she was always told by Nana.

*Have I ever done anything wrong enough to make you hate me?*

Laura wasn't sure.

She had sat in the hearse wearing a simple black dress with stockings that were quickly becoming unbearably itchy and hot. The skin around her thumb was irritated as she dug into it with her pointer finger, causing a new hangnail to appear. Maddy was looking down at her feet and scuffing her toes together, ruining her new shoes. Her father was standing outside of the long, black hearse, shaking hands and accepting condolences, in a black suit that hung around his waist and black shoes that stuck out from his draping pants like clown feet.

Laura and Maddy had stood in line with him for a while, thanking their family members and friends for coming to their mother's funeral. With every handclasp or sad smile, the heaviness of the air closed more deeply around her, until it seemed she was peering out from a dark cocoon.

*I can't take it anymore.*

"Come on, Maddy," Laura had said, grabbing Maddy's hand.

They had slipped into the back of the hearse, closing the door to muffle the sounds of sympathy from outside.

"Isn't it weird that we're just sitting in here?" Maddy had asked.

She'd always been scared of ghosts and death. The thought of death had never really frightened Laura.

*Life is finite. It has an end point. That's just a fact. It's kind of nice sitting here, so close to Mom.*

It was somehow comforting to know that her body was still an arm's length away, although hidden by layers of wood and embalmed.

"It's not weird to me," Laura had replied.

"Well, you're a freak, Laura," Maddy had said, shivering a little and turning away.

Her shoulders began to shudder slightly. She had placed a hand on Maddy's back, but Maddy turned further away and slid down the seat out of Laura's grasp.

*When will this be over? Funerals are the worst. They just make you feel sad, not better.*

Laura leaned her head against the seat, shut her eyes, and tried to block out the sound of Maddy's crying. In the nights of Maddy's baby years, her wails for milk always woke Laura up, too. Through teary sleep-filled eyes,

Laura would see a soft light appear in the hallway and the flimsy shadow of her mother drifting to Maddy's room. The crying would stop, and Laura would float back to sleep, comforted, even though her mother had not come to her.

Now here was her mother, pumped with chemicals, laying in a box, silent and staring from behind closed eyelids. Somehow, this was not a frightening thought for Laura. It was the same feeling she got when she looked out at the night sky and saw the many stars glittering deeply in the blackness. She felt so small, and the universe felt so large and impossible to fathom.

The shadow of the ash was growing long.

*Nearly nightfall. Dad's going to wonder where I am.*

It was quiet. The children had left to go home for dinner and the air was a little cooler. A breeze whipped her face. Stars were twinkling when Laura arrived back home. At the top of her long driveway, she slid to a stop, kicking up rough chunks of gravel and pebbles.

*Something's wrong.*

A large, white foreclosure sign with thick black letters had been hammered into the plump ground, soft with daily summer rain.

Laura jumped off of her bike, allowing it to bang on the hard blacktop, and ran up her driveway. The front door was ajar and hung crookedly. Its top hinge had been shaken loose, causing the door to hang at a diagonal. It looked like a slanted smile. A deep, banging noise that seemed to shake the whole house sounded every few moments.

Her father was stomping up and down the length of the kitchen and living room, yelling at no one, and waving his arms erratically. His eyes looked red, vacant, and hollow. In one hand, he was holding a bottle of beer that sloshed as he flailed. Every so often he would pause to punch the drywall with a hard fist, made stronger and more tolerant to pain, with the amount of alcohol he had consumed. Red blood streaked his knuckles.

"Dad, Dad, stop!" Laura cried.

The crooked door banged shut behind her. She ran to him and pulled on his beer-soaked shirt, trying to stop him, but it was like trying to tame a wild tiger. He continued to roar, now provoked even further. He rounded on her. Fire was in his eyes.

"Dad," Laura began to sob, "I tried to tell you."

It was now becoming very clear how adept her father was at placing problems into a closet in his mind and shutting the door against the accumulating mess. Letters from the bank had been arriving in the mail in the weeks prior. Laura had handed them to her father, but he always ripped them up and threw them in the garbage.

"This is all your fault," his voice dropped to a hoarse whisper and he took some stumbling steps closer to her.

"How is this my fault?" Laura cried.

*You are the one who made Mom's life hell, and now she's gone, and you're such a deadbeat that you can't even keep your own house.*

Laura swallowed the words and stared at her father, too angry to keep crying. He lunged at her, arms spread wide like a giant, lumbering bear on hind legs. The alcohol coursing through his bloodstream served to slow him down and prevent him from meeting his target. His open hands furiously grasped air as she ducked away and ran out the front door, down the stone steps, and past the pink and blue hydrangeas that her mother had planted, it seemed like an era ago, in the blooming days of Laura's infancy. With the blur of her childhood home behind her, Laura jumped onto her bike and began to pedal as hard as she could with no clear direction.

*The small white house of Laura's childhood had known her since the day she was born. It sat on a shady, green street in the suburbs. Tall trees lined the front edge of the property, and there was a small patch of forest directly behind the house. Large bushes and thick vines grew on either side, blocking out the noise and view of neighbors' lives.*

*"It was the best day of my life," Laura's mother had always said about Laura's birth. She loved to hear that, it was like being wrapped in a warm blanket.*

*"But why? Who wants to give birth on a bathroom floor?" Laura once asked.*

*"There are far worse things, my love."*

*Her mother said this with satisfaction and pride as if she had planned the birth that way instead of it surprising her. Having her baby come so quickly and without pain medication or medical intervention had sparked something inside of her. She became obsessed with healing and herbalism. Several shelves in their pantry were devoted to the many concoctions her mother had bought or made. The house smelled like a mix of flowers and dirt. It seemed at times that the outside had been brought in and was sprouting roots.*

*In some ways, her mother had been both far ahead of her time and also a relic of a distant past, when midwives had wrung hot, wet towels, drenched from water bubbling over a fire, and gathered herbs to calm swelling and staunch bleeding. When she was pregnant with Maddy, she sought out midwifery care and moved even more deeply away from the increasingly medicalized world. Laura later wondered if that was why, when she began having pain in her chest, she ignored it for so long until her large, loving heart became too full and marched to a complete stop.*

Laura arrived back home as the sky was turning a deep purple grey, and the stars were twinkling. The house was bathed in moonlight and shadows and seemed to breathe in the quiet dark, a deep exhale releasing its pain from earlier that day. Laura placed her bike against the garage under the overhang in case it rained, as her mother always used to remind her. Nana's car was in the driveway, having dropped off Maddy earlier.

*Guess she realized Dad was in no state to take care of Maddy.*

Laura walked inside, closing the broken door quietly behind her. Dirty dishes sat in the sink and the sound of distant snores echoed. Nana must have made Maddy dinner, closed her son's lolling jaw, rolled him on his side, and then finally moved her old, soft body onto the couch to keep a tired watch.

Laura stopped when she heard Maddy crying softly. Peering into her darkened bedroom, Laura saw her twisted in the sheets as if she had been trying to cocoon herself. She was holding a small stuffed animal, a bear that was once pink, but now had taken on a faint shade of brown, from many years of love. Without a word, Laura climbed into bed and wrapped herself around Maddy. The feeling of her small body, shuddering a bit, was comforting and she felt Maddy begin to soften until her breathing became slow and rhythmic.

*How did I get here? Must have stumbled out of Maddy's bed sometime in the night. Mmm breakfast, smells like bacon and maple syrup. Mom? Wait no, of course not, stupid. Nana's in the kitchen.*

The morning sun was just beginning to rise. Laura stood up slowly from her bed, feeling the muscles in her thin legs stretch long, and gazed out the window at the wash of yellow and green trees, standing like guardians. She dressed in a pair of jean shorts and a long, yellow tee-shirt that smelled like fresh laundry.

*Gotta remember to wash our clothes. Dad won't do it.*

Maddy and Nana were sitting at the kitchen table. Nana was sipping her coffee, black with sugar, and Maddy had a small mug of hot cocoa. The morning light continued to grow brighter, and the August heat filtered in, creating a warm dampness in the house.

Laura's father had left remnants of his tirade throughout the house like battle scars. Dark holes sat in the white painted drywall, portals that could suck her into another dimension if she peered into them closely enough, like the children in a beloved story, *The Lion, The Witch, and The Wardrobe.*

"And Charlie Brown's teacher said 'wah, wah, wah," Nana said, reading aloud the cartoon page from the newspaper.

Maddy laughed, mostly at Nana's twisted, funny face as she spoke gibberish.

Heavy footsteps sounded suddenly from further down the hall.

*Goddamnit, he's up.*

Laura leapt inside, feeling her rib cage jolt as the footsteps grew closer and louder. Her hands clenched into small fists. Bending her head, Laura grabbed a plate from the dishwasher, walked over to the stove, and began to scoop pancakes and eggs from the stained baking sheet Nana had laid out on top of the stove.

Silence draped the kitchen as her father stepped in. Nana's lilting voice halted and Maddy's smile straightened. Laura crawled into the furthest corner of her mind.

*Wouldn't it be great if those holes actually were portals and I could be whisked away to another place and time?*

"Jacob," Nana suddenly said, twisting her body away from the table and looking over her shoulder.

Long ago, her hair had been a deep, rich, red color, but in the last couple of decades had begun to show more and more tendrils of white. Nana's solution to aging was a bottle of Clairol that made her hair the color of dry autumn leaves.

"Leave it, Mom," he growled in a voice thick with sleep and the physical exhaustion of drinking too much, too often. Nana turned back around, shaking her head.

Laura's father began to serve himself breakfast, and she ducked away from the stove, avoiding coming within several feet of her father.

Timidly, she announced, "I'm going to go eat breakfast in my room."

Without looking up from the stove her father replied gruffly, "No. You're not."

He was still wearing the same stained shirt from the day before, and the smell of sweat and booze lingered around him.

*Okay, fine.*

Laura sat down at the kitchen table. Every time she tried to eat, the food seemed to come back up her throat so that she never knew if she was chewing or swallowing.

Her father sat down across from her, his head still bowed. For such a large man, he always ate very slowly and carefully. Not a fleck of food on his plate was wasted, and every morsel was cut and distributed to his mouth with what always seemed like painstaking care. As he emerged from his meal, he leaned back in his chair, took a napkin, and slowly wiped his mouth while staring at Laura. The grease from the butter stained his napkin a pale yellow.

His gaze felt heavy and full of thought. "You need to begin packing up all your stuff. I have boxes in the garage that you can use. I'm going out today before work to look for a new place for us to stay until things clear up."

*Things clear up? Our house is gone. This isn't an afternoon thunderstorm that will pass in an hour.*

"Jacob, whatever you need, I'm here to help you," Nana said, but she didn't meet her son's eyes.

Her gaze was fixed on her granddaughters. Laura's father didn't reply. He pushed back the kitchen chair, allowing it to scrape along the wood, something that had always irritated Laura's mother. He filled a mug with coffee, black and bitter. Banging the unhinged door behind him, left the house without a goodbye or an acknowledgment of the women who stood watching him.

# August 1999

The air was hinting at coolness and the leaves on the trees were not quite green, but not yet the golden color of fall, when Laura, Maddy, and their father packed the last few boxes into his red station wagon and drove out of the long driveway for the last time. Maddy turned around in her seat, climbed onto her knees, and pressed her freckled nose into the water-stained back windshield.

*Don't do it, don't turn around and look. Okay, maybe just a quick glance.*

Laura twisted around, looking at the small brown house, shaded by many trees. The gardens that her mother had cared for painstakingly had grown long this year, and the grass in the front yard was brown. No one had cared for these plants, and now the land the house sat on was left to its own wildness until someone new came to care for it, hopefully with the same love it had been shown for so many years.

Laura found that she didn't have the urge to cry, as she thought she would. Instead, she had a vision, clear as day. The front yard was in full bloom, her mother was sitting on the front porch in a white rocker, holding Maddy to her breast, and she was about seven, running exuberantly through the yard holding a kite. The vision appeared as a still life, a captured moment that flashed in front of her eyes as if she were looking at an old photograph. It was so happy and full of joy that Laura found herself smiling, lost for a moment. The station wagon hit a pothole and the vision evaporated.

"Well, that's it. A lifetime of hard work down the toilet," her father mumbled, half to himself.

He opened his window and flicked the end of his cigarette onto the street. Then, he brought the cigarette to his mouth, breathed in, and exhaled with a deep sigh. Laura looked out of her window, clutching a box of Maddy's stuffed animals in her arms. Maddy had not wanted to part with them, even though their father had already transported most of their belongings to the new apartment. When Laura had tried to pack up her stuffed animals, Maddy had clung to them viciously. Now, they were in boxes in the back seat of the wagon, threatening to smother Laura with their dusty, stained fur. Maddy was hugging a bear, purple with a missing eye, that she had named Mommy Bear since their mother had died.

The streets became less wooded, denser with people and shops, as they drove through the main part of town. Past the taller buildings and men in business suits, until they reached the winding side streets close to the coast, filled with old houses built shoulder to shoulder many years ago, now run-down. Some had peeling paint or crooked stairs. Others had chain link fences and tiny yards with barking dogs. They took a few more side streets, drawing even closer to the coast. When Laura looked out of the window at the sky, she could see gulls floating in the breeze.

The red wagon came to a stop in front of a yellow duplex.

*Wait, is that our new home? It's yellow. Maybe yellow doesn't even describe it. It's more mustard with a skim of bile green. Gross. That's some shoddy paint job. And it's on Peaceful Street, such an ironic name for a drab little road on the decrepit edges of Connecticut. What a sick joke.*

The steps leading up to the house were wooden, cracked, and worn and the window frames were unpainted. A few were falling apart, rotting from the outside in.

Laura sat for a moment in the wagon.

*I cannot be the person who lives here. I'm not the person who would live in a house like that. But, who would that person actually be?*

All of a sudden everything seemed hysterically funny. Her belly began to shudder with laughter. She had to hold her cheeks and bite her lip to keep from breaking into peals of hysteria. Her father was sitting in the front seat, finishing his cigarette, and reading over the lease agreement one more time.

"Damn thieves," he said. "They promised they'd fix those windows."

He unbuckled his seatbelt, stepped out of the car, and strode toward the house, taking a few moments to examine the windows and steps.

"I'll be damned if they fix these now I've signed the papers," he said.

"Daddy, you should have gotten the agreement in writing," Laura said as she climbed out of the car.

Maddy stood and joined them, just as Nana's car drove up. Nana had rented out her one bedroom apartment across town so that she could stay in the duplex and help their father. She said that she would live there for a few months.

*She's going to be stuck with us, like it or not, for years.*

Nana had a sense of duty and responsibility to her family that was borne from obligation rather than love and kindness. She was of an iron generation who, when a need was seen, did not hesitate to help despite personal sacrifice.

The gray clouds above now threatened rain with a chilly dampness, and Laura's father turned up his jacket collar and bent his head down. Age was creeping up on his face. In pictures from their old house, he appeared to be a different person long ago, jovial, full of light, and excited for life. Laura had always loved one in particular, a picture of him sweeping her mother off of her feet on their wedding day. The photo was candid, she could tell by the look of surprise in her mother's eyes and the devilish grin on her father's face. No wedding photographer could have made that happen. It was in black and white, and Laura loved looking at it. It was tucked into a silver frame, and behind it, Laura's mother had pressed a single white lily, now faded brown, from her wedding day. It was like a relic from an ancient time, before care and drinking had whittled her father down to a shadow of the young man he once was.

Before they had left the house, she had made sure to take that photo and wrap it carefully in Maddy's old baby rags, and then she cradled it in a box with her own pillows and blankets.

*I'll keep it in my underwear drawer in our new bedroom, that way no one will ruin it.*

Droplets started to fall from the sky as Laura's father searched for the right key on his ring. Laura, Maddy, and Nana stood stiffly watching him fumble.

"Damn keys," her father muttered.

He fiddled with the house key, trying to push it into the lock. With a few jabs, he was able to secure it, and then he twisted the old doorknob, finally pushing in the front door with a heave. The door was painted red, a horrible color against the moldy yellow, and as it flung open, seemingly against its will, splinters rained down on them.

"That's better than it was the first time," her father said, using his jacket sleeve to brush away more cobwebs and wood remnants.

Nana coughed a few times from the dust and Maddy had a look of horror in her eyes, but Laura knew that she was too afraid to complain. She held her bear a little tighter and stepped into the main living area. Laura followed, and then Nana stepped in, holding a flowered handkerchief across her nose and mouth.

The inside of the apartment wasn't much better than the outside. It had a dank smell of wetness and something like old cat litter. The carpet in the entryway and living room was dark brown, likely hiding many decades of dirt and grime. Peeling yellow wallpaper covered the walls in some areas and dark wood paneling in others. The paneling gave the illusion that you were stepping into a wooden box with a lid fitted tight. To the right, there was a kitchen painted blue with yellow linoleum floors and a broken faux Tiffany chandelier hanging askew. To the left was a short hallway that led to a bathroom and three bedrooms.

"Home, sweet home," Laura's father said sarcastically.

He had brought over some of their old furniture that would fit in the new place. The cream-colored chenille couch passed down from her mother's mother who had died many years ago, sat on top of the dirty brown rug. Two carved wooden end tables flanked the couch, and their coffee table, a rich mahogany, sat in front. The television sat on a chest of drawers. To the right of the couch, Nana's favorite chair from her apartment sat, awaiting its evening ritual of Wheel of Fortune and drips of chocolate pudding, spilled on it. Laura could see their table and chairs from home sitting in the kitchen.

*Dad must have put our beds in the back bedroom already.*
*At least we still have the furniture, even if it looks completely ridiculous.*
*What would Mom think of all this?*

The furniture, at least, was some sort of anchor to the person she was. Walking toward the chenille sofa, she ran her hand against its soft back.

*Don't cry.*

Maddy had already ran to their bedroom with her stuffed animals to begin setting up her bed, and Nana was in her room laying out her clothing, deciding exactly how to organize her things in such a limited space.

Laura's father had followed Nana into the back, and she could hear them talking. Nana's voice sounded strained. She leaned against the couch, listening.

"Jacob, I know you don't want to hear this, but this is not a place for children," she said.

"Mom, there's nothing I can do. Do you think I want this?"

"I don't know what you want, and I wish I could help you more, get you and the girls out of this," she paused, "hovel."

"It's only for a time, hopefully just a few months until I can get my feet back on the ground, maybe find a second job, get a better place," his voice trailed off.

There was a pause that felt heavy and complicated. "I'm going to head out, make a few stops before work. I'll see you later."

Laura stepped into the kitchen, pretending to look through the cabinets to hide the fact that she had been listening.

*Then again this place is so small it would be hard to have a private conversation.*

Her father left without saying goodbye, slamming the splintered door hard behind him, and stepping into the drizzle.

*I know exactly where those "few stops" are. The one good thing about this move for Dad is that he's much closer to his beloved watering holes. I'm going to be stuck here forever, imprisoned by a drunk.*

# September 1999

Laura dressed slowly in the dark, to not wake Maddy. The night before, she had picked out her outfit for the first day of ninth grade. Laura looked in the mirror at her shadowy figure. The September light was just beginning to brighten the room, and in the grayness, her pink dress and white tights looked dull, even dirty. Laura sighed and straightened the skirt of her dress. It was an outfit her mother had bought her last year for a trip to the theater in New York City.

*The lights of the stage were so bright, reflecting off of the actors' and actresses' wet mouths open in song. Mom told me how beautiful I looked. She did my hair in a French braid.*

The playbill from the show, Oklahoma, was still nestled in her memory box. She had placed the box in the top shelf of her closet for safekeeping, burying the remnants of her former life, only to be taken out occasionally, she promised herself.

She began to brush her long hair.

*Dad will kill me if I try to put makeup on, even though all the other girls started wearing makeup in sixth grade. Mom told me I could wear makeup in high school, just not too much. Dad will go into a tirade if I put on the slightest hint of eyeshadow, and I can't stomach that right now. I don't even want to go to school and face all these people.*

Laura took one more look in the mirror and then walked out of the room, slowly closing the door to prevent the squeaking hinges from waking Maddy. Her father was in the kitchen, making coffee. His graying hair was uncombed and stuck out in fluffy tufts around his ears, like the soft under-feathers of a bird. This gave him a slightly maniacal look, coupled with his thick reading glasses that magnified his eyes. He greeted her with a slight grunt and glanced at her briefly.

"What are you wearing that for?" he asked. "It's so... fancy."

"It's the first day of school," she shrugged, avoiding eye contact.

Laura grabbed a brown sugar Pop-Tart from the cabinet and made her way quickly to the front door to put on her backpack.

*Luckily, the bus will pick me up a few blocks away from my house, so none of the other kids will know that I live here.*

When she had discovered this last week, the relief she felt was so strong that she thought she would faint.

Her father eyed her darkly, a storm brewing in his mind.

*This dress is appropriate, Mom picked it out. What's he going to say now?*

Yes, Laura was starting to develop. The dress that had hung loosely around her body last year now clung. In the last year, her hips had widened, and there was a gentle sway to her back. Her breasts were small but noticeable. Her father's eyes felt heavy and penetrating. Laura's discomfort was palpable, like a small seed of disgust planted in her stomach.

Laura grabbed the door handle, closing the door on her father's wordless stare. And with a few swift jerks, opened it and stepped into the morning. She walked the few blocks to the bus stop, tugging on the straps of her backpack, stomach growling.

Up ahead, Laura could see a small group of students gathered on the corner. Some parents were waiting with their kids, and one mom was smoking a cigarette a little further away from the group. She recognized a few of the kids, but couldn't place any of the faces with names.

*At least they're like me, stuck in this dumpy part of town, probably embarrassed even to be seen together.*

Laura walked up to the group and hung on the edge, toeing the ground with her Mary-Janes and listening for the sound of squeaking brakes to arrive. The other kids didn't even notice that she had arrived.

*Better to go unnoticed.*

None of the girls she had once called friends had biked to her house, rang her doorbell, asked to hang out, or called her house since she had moved in May. This was both heartbreaking and comforting--she wouldn't have to search them out and explain anything to them.

*Hopefully if I do pass them in the hallway, they'll just look through me, like a ghost.*

"Hey," a voice, a girl's voice, but somewhat deep and commanding, drew Laura out of her reverie.

Laura, startled, looked up. She must have had a blank expression on her face because the girl waved at her with a questioning look on her face.

"Hey, are you okay?"

"Yeah, yeah," Laura replied. She tried to smile. "Just thinking."

At that moment, a flash of yellow appeared in the corner of Laura's eye, and the familiar squeal of brakes sounded.

"Bus is here," Laura said, pointing.

"Yeah, it is," the girl replied.

She was still looking at Laura, smiling, barely acknowledging the arrival of the school bus. Laura took a few steps forward, and the girl continued to stare at her.

*Why the hell is she staring at me?*

"Okay, well, I'm going to head in," Laura said, feeling awkward at the intensity of the girl's stare. The last of the students were filing into the bus, climbing the steps that Laura had always thought were made for a giant.

"Right, you first," the girl replied.

She stood behind Laura now, a little too close. Laura could see that she was wearing a pair of faded jeans, and the knees were just beginning to rip. She had a long sweater plastered with the faces of some boy band. Her hair was dark brown and held high with a ponytail holder. A poof of bangs emerged from the top of her head and they were fluffed up with lots of hair spray. So much hair spray that, at this close proximity, Laura could smell the chemical halo that lingered around her head.

*Make yourself as small as possible.*

The smell of the bus, sweat, plastic, and fuel, was familiar. She imagined herself sinking into the vinyl floor, hiding under one of the seats, so that she would not have to face the eyes of the students looking at her as she boarded. A couple of kids had turned to whisper to each other.

*Ugh, they probably recognize me.*

Her school wasn't small, but everyone seemed to know everything about everyone.

*Please, please don't let them find out where I live now.*

The girl behind her was still close and seemed to be following her to the back of the bus, to an open seat two rows from the back door. Laura slid into the brown, plastic bus bench that was somehow always sticky and smelled of sneakers. The girl with the boy band sweater sat down beside Laura, pulling off her black backpack, stuck with pins from other bands that Laura didn't recognize, and turned to her with her big grin.

"Hey," she said again.

"Hey," Laura repeated, her stomach sinking.

*This girl must be following me to ask questions about Mom.*

"Are you new here, too?"

*New? Maybe there's hope. She doesn't know me.*

"No, I've lived in this town my whole life, I just moved to this side over the summer," Laura replied.

"Oh, I thought you were new when I saw you hanging out not talking to anyone at the bus stop. I just moved here from California with my mom. My grandma lives around here, and my dad left us a few months ago, so my mom wanted to go somewhere close to family," she said nonchalantly.

*That's an awful lot of information to share with a stranger, but at least she really doesn't know who I am. Better to just let her keep talking.*

Laura reached into her backpack and grabbed the Pop-Tart from the outside pocket.

"Oh, can I have some?" the girl asked.

"Uh, yeah, sure," Laura replied, taken aback by her request.

*Who asks a stranger to share their breakfast?*

However, there was something earnest and genuine in the way she spoke. Laura thought that she should be annoyed, and with anyone else she might have been, but instead, she felt intrigued. She broke off half of the Pop-Tart and handed it to the girl.

"Thanks," the girl said, spraying brown sugar crumbs in Laura's direction. "What's your name?"

"Laura, what's yours?

"Samantha, but I hate that name. Everyone calls me Sammy," she smiled. "Hey, do you like N*Sync?" She pulled on her sweater to show Laura the faces on the front.

"Um, not really," said Laura. "Well, I don't really know much about them."

"You don't know N*Sync? Where have you been?"

"My dad doesn't really let me listen to that music. And, we don't have cable."

Sammy rolled her eyes.

"Listen, you're coming to my house. My mom works all the time, so she doesn't know what I watch. And even if she did, she wouldn't care," she shrugged.

"Wow, your mom sounds cool."

"She is, she's like my best friend. Hey, we're here!"

The red brick of the high school loomed through the windshield of the bus. When Laura was little and they would drive by the high school, she always thought that it looked like a castle, and she couldn't wait to walk through its big, red front doors. Now, on the first day of ninth grade, it looked more like a fortress.

*Would anyone notice if I just ran off this bus, and hid in the trees forever?*

"Are you okay?" Sammy asked.

Laura gulped and looked at Sammy as if she were emerging from a dream. "Oh, yeah, sorry."

"You keep zoning out," Sammy said.

"Just first day of school nerves I guess."

Laura stood in line, single file, to exit the bus, and saw the sea of high-schoolers swarming the entryway below. It looked like a very busy ant farm. Everyone seemed to know exactly what to do and where to go. Shouts, whistles, and joyful greetings sounded from the student body, and Laura wanted more than ever to crawl into a very tiny hole and disappear altogether.

"What teacher do you have for Homeroom?" asked Sammy.

"Um, Mrs. Snyder," Laura replied.

"Me, too!" she squealed with a big thumbs up.

They began to exit the bus and walk toward the school. A wave of nausea. Just a few steps ahead were Tina and Lindsey, girls she had known since they were all in diapers. When her mother died in the spring, their mothers had phoned her house and spoken briefly to her father, but she hadn't seen or heard from her friends since then.

*Wow, they've really gone all out for the first day of school.*

Their hair was streaked with color and blown out. Their jeans were both Jordache brand, and they looked identical.

Laura imagined the shopping trip they must have gone on together to pick out those outfits. She pictured them sitting on Tina's four-poster bed with the white lace duvet, flipping through magazines, and planning how to do their hair. Laura knew that one thing was on their mind: boys.

In middle school, they had all shared their crushes in an innocent, childish way. They would stay up late into the night at sleepovers, analyzing what their first kiss would be like. Something had changed at the end of eighth grade, though. The conversations seemed less like a fairy-tale, and more raw somehow. Lindsey and Tina seemed to suddenly grow up as if someone had pressed the fast-forward button on puberty. Lindsey was especially developed, and she would look in the mirror, slide red lipstick on her lips, often hitting her teeth, press her breasts together, and ask Laura and Tina if she should buy a push-up bra. Laura had been the least developed of the three of them. She wasn't entirely comfortable with their sudden talk of sex and push-up bras. Part of her wanted to stay locked away in fairy-tale land.

Lindsey and Tina's fantasy worlds had evolved to first dates, kissing in cars, and ended with curious and detailed conversations about sex. Laura's dreams were simpler. She imagined a handsome boy, usually faceless, with long, blonde hair sweeping her off her feet at a school dance, the night ending with a chaste kiss.

The chasm between her and Lindsey and Tina had only widened once her mother had died. And looking at them, standing in front of her, laughing loudly with their hands on their hips, she realized that they had changed into teenagers over the summer, while she had remained locked into little girlhood. A sense of loneliness so deep that she had to suppress a sob overcame her suddenly, and she disguised the gasp as a cough, as she pretended to look through her backpack for her schedule.

"This is so different from L.A.," Sammy was saying, as they filed into the big red doors. They looked like an open mouth, turned sideways.

"First of all, your weather sucks. Second, everything is so much more relaxed out there. When I think of the East Coast, all I hear is rules, rules, rules."

"You're not wrong," Laura said.

*So, so many rules. It must feel good to break them.*

Lindsey and Tina were not far ahead, and Laura knew that soon they would be walking in step with them to the ninth grade wing. She kept glancing at them, trying to slow her steps to widen the gap. It was to no avail, and as she rounded the corner of the ninth grade hallway with Sammy, she found herself shoulder to shoulder with Tina. Tina did a double-take, looking over at Laura, flipping her blonde hair out of her face.

"Oh, Laura, hi!" she exclaimed too excitedly.

Her smile was stretched too wide and didn't extend to her eyes, which were caked with blue eyeshadow and Maybelline mascara.

*Maybe she's born with it...but probably not.*

Tina pulled Laura in for a hug, and she could smell her drugstore perfume. Lindsey looked at Laura with sympathetic, puppy-dog eyes.

*Oh no, here it comes.*

"We're so sorry about what happened," Lindsey said.

"Yeah, we really are," Tina echoed.

The words came crashing down over Laura like a giant wave. They swept her up and spit her out somewhere far away from ninth grade.

"Oh, thanks," she heard someone mutter.

The words must have come out of her, but she didn't feel her mouth moving.

Tina and Lindsey gave one more identical half-smile, and then they were swept away in another wave, carried down the hallway with the rest of the ninth graders, engulfed once more in their own little sadness's and longings.

"What was that about?" Sammy's loud voice shattered Laura's reverie.

"We were friends last year," Laura said. "Before my mom died."

There was a deep pause.

"Oh, wow!" Sammy exclaimed. "I am so sorry."

She came to a full stop in the moving sea of students. A couple of kids pushed past her.

One muttered, "What the hell, watch where you're going," and Sammy replied by flipping up her middle finger at him with a wide, sarcastic smile.

Sammy placed her hands on Laura's shoulders and looked Laura in the eyes.

"That sucks so bad," she said with the most genuine concern that Laura had heard from anyone. Sammy wrapped Laura in a tight hug.

*Everyone's staring, but who cares.*

It felt so good to have this strange girl hug her. She squinted her eyes open and saw N*Sync staring back at her. Something inside of her that had been shut tight since May unlocked. Sammy was the first to pull away.

"Come on, let's go," Sammy said, grabbing Laura's hand.

They rejoined the flow of students like droplets in an unfathomable ocean.

# November 1999

The sun was already low, casting long shadows through hazy clouds over the swing set in the park where Laura and Sammy went every day after school. Laura had found herself in the midst of a social circle that, had her mom not died, she probably never would have associated herself with. Somehow, in the last two months, she fit with the misfits. The feeling was new but not uncomfortable.

The park next to the school was their hangout. She would slip out of class as soon as the bell rang, grab her backpack, and run out the red front doors to meet Sammy on the sidewalk. They would jump over the fence on the north side of the school, the quickest way to get there, and laugh and gossip about their teachers and other students until they found themselves amidst trees and grass on the far side of the town park. It was always quiet there.

Now, the trees were bare and made a crackling sound in the dry autumn wind. Sometimes Jane would follow them through the trees behind the school, over the fence, and to the park. She had made friends with Sammy in art class. Laura didn't like her very much. Jane always called herself an artist in a way that made Laura want to roll her eyes. She also had a weird obsession with vampires, wore black a lot, and always had heavy eyeliner on. Whenever Sammy would crack a joke, Jane would laugh without a smile. Laura wasn't sure how this was possible, but it frightened her a little. Sammy didn't seem bothered by her, but Laura always felt like she needed a long shower after spending time with Jane.

Jane lived close to Laura, but in a house even more ramshackle than Laura's duplex. The one time Laura had seen it, it had looked like a haunted house, and it seemed fitting that someone like Jane would emerge from it.

On this chilly November day, Laura, Sammy, and Jane huddled together trying to stay warm. Jane was showing Laura and Sammy some charcoal drawings from her art portfolio, and Sammy was nodding and smiling.

*Her drawings are pretty good but so creepy. Why does Sammy like that sort of thing?*

"What's that?" asked Laura.

Jane had put her portfolio to the side as she pulled something out of her backpack.

Jane smirked. She looked at Laura and held the little baggie up to her face.

"It's weed, pot, Mary Jane, whatever you want to call it."

"Why do you have it?" Laura asked.

"My older brother smokes it all the time. I thought that I'd grab a little for us to try." Jane's eyes were shining.

"I tried it once, in California," Sammy said. "I coughed a lot. I also saw some weird shit." Her ponytail brushed her cheek as she laughed and looked at Jane. "I don't think weed is supposed to do that."

"It was probably your imagination, you idiot," Jane said.

She pulled out a white piece of paper and gingerly placed a small amount of the green substance into it. Then she began to carefully roll it. Laura noticed that her skin was very pale and there was grey and brown dirt beneath her fingernails.

"Jane, we're going to get caught!" Laura hissed.

*Okay, calm down, don't be a freak.*

Jane rolled her eyes. "Laura, there's no one here. Don't be such a loser."

Sammy met Laura's eyes but didn't say anything. It was true that no one was around. The only people Laura could see on this chilly day were a few boys kicking around a soccer ball in a far-off field, and a mom with her son on the swings, almost out of view.

"Here, if it makes you feel better, let's face this way." Sammy turned toward the woods and Laura and Jane turned too.

Jane pulled a blue lighter out of her backpack and lit the rolled joint. The spark flashed for a second and then the tip glowed a burnt orange. A thin stream of smoke slowly poured from the end. Jane brought the joint up to her lips and inhaled deeply. She held her breath for a moment and then exhaled the smoke high into the air. Laura saw wisps of it floating off into the gray sky.

"I'll try that," Sammy said.

She held out her hand for the joint, and Jane passed it to her with a sly, satisfied smile playing around her lips. It was clear that Jane enjoyed breaking the rules, but perhaps even more than that, she relished pulling the others into delinquency. Sammy leaned back on her hands and pointed her chin upward, allowing the effects of the smoke to settle into her brain.

"Your turn, Laura," Jane said with the same smile.

*Be cool, don't show you're nervous. You just got a new group of friends, right? Don't blow it.*

Laura took the joint and pressed it against her lips. She took a tiny breath in, and tasted the acrid smoke swirling through her mouth. She tried again, this time breathing more deeply.

*Not so bad.*

Laura coughed a little, and then fully exhaled the remainder of smoke, as if she were holding a high note. A sense of warmth and cloudiness descended upon her brain that was not unpleasant. She looked around at her friends.

*Sammy's eyes are ringed with red, and she's talking about something, but I can't follow her words.*

They seemed to be moving either too quickly or too slowly, she wasn't sure which. Laura laid down on the cold, hard ground. Sammy joined her and grabbed her hand. Jane was busy puffing on the joint.

"Do you ever think about your mom?" Sammy whispered.

*Do we really have to talk about this now?*

"Yeah," Laura nodded but didn't turn her head to look at Sammy.

"I've heard people say they can feel their relatives after they die. Like, they feel like there's someone in the room with them, or they smell their perfume. Does that ever happen to you?"

Laura shook her head, no.

"I bet, if you tried, you could feel her," Sammy said.

Laura closed her eyes and listened. The sound of Jane's hoarse cough was muffled by the wind, now growing stronger. The dull roar of a plane sounded overhead.

*I remember Mom's arms, wrapped around me while I fell asleep. The sound of her laughter. Other people might have thought she had an annoying laugh, too loud. I loved it. Mom?*

Laura peered into the foggy gray above, but no ghostly outline appeared.

All she sensed was Sammy's cold hand. It grounded her.

"No, no I can't feel her."

"Well, maybe with more time, who knows," Sammy replied, looking up into the same gray sky.

Laura knew that no one close to Sammy had ever died, but sometimes she did talk about her dad leaving. From what she said, it seemed like the same void had opened for her as well and never fully shut.

Jane had extinguished the joint and was packing up her backpack. She was bent over arranging her books, and Laura could see a faint spray of dandruff in her stringy black hair.

"Hey, let's go back to my house," Jane said, looking up.

"My mom's out until 9, and I have some more of this," she held up the baggie once again and waved it in Laura's face with an evil smile.

"Thanks, but I have to head home," Laura said, gathering her backpack, too. "My dad's home from work early tonight, and I can't be late."

"Yeah, I'd come over, but my mom left meatballs in the fridge and I'm getting hungry. Hey, Laura, when can I come over to your house? I want to meet your family," Sammy said, standing up.

Laura shook her head and avoided eye contact.

"No, you don't," she said.

"I do. And I want to see where you live."

"Some other time. My dad doesn't like me having friends over after school."

"Okay," she shrugged. "It's getting cold, let's race to the fence," Sammy said. She began to run at a fast clip, her sweatshirt hood flapping a bit in the breeze that stirred around her.

"You go on, I'm no runner," called Jane.

The haziness of the weed was lifting from Laura's brain, and as she began to run, she felt the cold wind sharp against her cheeks.

"I win," yelled Sammy, throwing her hands above her head and dancing a little.

Her cheeks were stained rosy with cold. Laura and Sammy stepped out of the park and began to walk south, toward the coast and the woebegone houses that littered its edges. As they walked, the sky began to darken and the first glimmer of Christmas lights shone in some of the stores. They passed the small bodega with the friendly owner who had a long black mustache and always let them take one free piece of candy. As they walked past the police station, Sammy rubbed her eyes and walked a little straighter. Silence surrounded them. The life of the evening sprung up around them. The second act of a play. Daylight, then a brief intermission as the sun set, and then the final act in artificially lit darkness.

*What had life been like before electricity? How quiet it must have been, how dark and shadowy.*

There had been a documentary shown in school in fifth grade that had actors dressed up in clothing from the 1700s. They wore long dresses, and the women had to have their hair tied back unless they were bathing or sleeping. Laura absentmindedly stroked her long hair.

*How horrible to have to hide it. Who had decided that women should do that? It must have been the choice of their fathers or grandfathers.*

Laura shuddered to think of the control men had over a choice as simple as whether to wear your hair up, tied tight, or down, sweeping around your shoulders, back, maybe touching your waist.

*Dad's one of those men, who would have made that rule, and many more rules. If I'd lived way back then, I would've let my hair down, lit a joint, and stomped around in men's clothing.*

At least, she hoped she would have been like that.

They reached the street where they had to part ways. They gave each other a brief hug, and then Laura turned down her street. She glanced behind her once to look at Sammy walking away, her backpack bumping a little as she walked. Laura wrapped her sweater tightly.

*Should have dressed better for a late November evening.*

Laura turned into her yard, opened the metal gate, and clicked it shut behind her. The family that lived on the other side of their duplex was cooking dinner, and Laura could smell the scent of Vietnamese food wafting from their windows, cracked open slightly. The sound of small children playing also floated out. Laura walked up to her red door and pulled it open. Her father's car was parked on the sidewalk outside of the house, and as she stepped inside she could hear him speaking loudly to Nana.

*Oh no, what now?*

Maddy was doing her math homework in the kitchen, her cheek resting on her hand, as she chewed the side of a pencil, seemingly unperturbed by the noise. Laura's hands felt icy, so she walked over to the stove where Nana was baking something. Opening the oven door slightly, she placed her hands in the exhalation of warm air.

The voices in the back began to escalate.

"Hey, Maddy, what are you working on?" She asked, trying to ignore them.

"Fractions," Maddy replied.

Laura could hear the eye roll in her voice.

"What's Nana making for dinner?"

"I think it's a meatloaf."

"What are Dad and Nana talking about?" Laura asked.

"I don't know...the rent?" Maddy said, not looking up. "Can you stop asking so many questions?" Her voice was tense.

The broken chandelier above the kitchen table cast a gloomy yellow light across Maddy's bent head.

"Sorry, you don't have to snap."

Laura walked down the hallway and over to Nana's bedroom. She bent her ear toward the door, which was slightly open, and listened.

"Jacob, I can give you the money, I have it if you need it," she heard Nana say.

"Mom, I told you I don't need your money," her father replied.

His voice was dripping with alcohol.

"Well, Laura and Maddy need new clothes for the winter. Especially Maddy, she's growing like a weed. Just let me help, that's what I'm here for," Nana pleaded.

"I said no!" Her father shouted.

Laura heard something crash in the bedroom, and she rushed in. Her father had knocked over the floor lamp by Nana's bed. As it fell, it had hit the dresser, and caused a picture of Nana and Laura's Grampy to fall down. Her father swayed a little where he stood, almost unaware of the lamp and the picture. His eyes turned toward Laura, recognizing her shape out of the corner of his eye.

"Were you eavesdropping?" He rounded on her, taking a few stumbling steps forward.

Grabbing her chin sharply, he yanked her face up to look in his. His skin had stubble like small, black needles, and the scent of whiskey was musky on his breath.

"Jacob, stop, you'll hurt the child," Nana called from across the room. Out of the corner of Laura's eye, she could see Nana holding onto the bed.

*She's frightened.*

"Were you?" Her father hissed in her face.

Laura tried to shake her head.

"No, no," she said. "I heard the crash and wanted to make sure everything was okay."

Her father released her chin with a jerk, causing her neck to twist in an unnatural way. He stood up tall, looking at both his mother and daughter.

"You both think I'm a screw-up, right?"

There was silence.

*Of course, you're a screw-up. You made Mom's life hell and now you're making our lives hell.*

Laura swallowed these words.

"Isn't that right?" He roared, flecks of spit dotting Laura's face.

He took the floor lamp that had fallen against the dresser in both hands and then heaved it into the wall, causing the cheap metal lamp to bend and crumple. Laura crossed the room to stand next to Nana, shaking.

Laura's father turned around, facing them.

"I'm done with all of you," he spit out the words with disgust.

With heavy feet, he turned, stomping down the hallway to the entryway. Laura heard the jingle of keys and the slam of the broken door. Nana sat down on the edge of the bed with her hands clasped tightly in prayer, as if squeezing her hands harder would make her prayers louder. She rocked back and forth as tears poured out of her eyes.

*No God I know would take my mother and leave me with this man as a father, so why pray for anything?*

Maddy was sitting at the kitchen table where Laura had left her, her face white and ghostly. Laura sat down beside her and held her hand.

*He never turns on Maddy, maybe because she's the baby.*

Laura was thankful for that, and she clasped her hand because she needed the comfort maybe even more than Maddy needed comforting.

She looked over at the stove and saw a line of smoke was streaming from the oven door that she had left open.

*Crap, the meatloaf!*

It was blackened on top and somehow smelled like burnt rubber.

*Shit.*

Turning off the oven, she took the meatloaf out quickly and carefully cut off the burnt top.

*I don't even feel like eating.*

As she placed the utensils next to the plates, she had to hold the edge of the table to keep her legs from shaking.

"Here, Maddy, I'm not hungry tonight. You can have this while you watch TV," Laura said, handing her a plate.

She bounded over to the couch and curled up, seemingly forgetting everything that had just happened.

*Wow, is that just Maddy or are all kids so resilient?*

The hum of the television and the sound of Maddy eating was comforting for Laura. She walked down the hallway and peeked into Nana's bedroom. Nana was now clasping a rosary and muttering a quiet prayer.

*It must suck to have a son who's a drunk. It sucks having a drunk dad, but it must be even harder to have a drunk son. It must always feel like your fault.*

She walked to her bedroom and sat down in front of the vanity, brushing her hair with the copper brush that had belonged to her mother's mother. The ritual was peaceful and calming, and Laura's nervous system gradually returned to a relaxed state. She gazed at the mirror as she brushed her hair, but she was afraid to look herself in the eyes. Raised red marks had appeared on her chin where her father had grabbed her.

*I can't look quite yet.*

In her desk drawer, there was a small pot of powder makeup, and she would wear that in the morning to cover the yellow and blue bruises that were in the shape of fingerprints.

# December 1999

Nana walked with short hurried steps, holding Maddy's hand, as they whisked through the crowded mall. She always wore low heels, and even with the roar of noise, they clicked sharply on the tiled floor. Holiday shoppers flowed through the aisles and corridors, sometimes creating a jam so tight they had to pause their steps and wait for the crowd ahead to untangle itself.

Nana was all business, not stopping to browse or chat, methodically crossing off each item on her list. A film of sweat glossed Laura's skin underneath her winter jacket, and heat seemed to emanate from her back, creating a fog of unpleasant warmth.

Usually, Laura enjoyed the mall decorations, but this year the spectacle was nauseating. Animatronic Santa Clauses with red felt suits and woolen beards seemed to dot each store window, waving their robot arms at passersby. Smiling elves with rosy cheeks peeked sneakily around displays of clothing and toys. Large white, sparkling snowflakes hung from strings from the vaulted ceiling, and in the center of the mall, a huge fake tree stood with colored lights flashing manically.

Already that day they had traipsed through several stores, purchasing candles for their teachers, and a blue sweater for their father.

*Drenched with alcohol-laced vomit soon, I'm sure. I still need a small present for Sammy.*

Nana and Maddy were getting more annoying as the shopping trip went on, but Laura didn't know why. A hot, bubbling sensation was brewing in her stomach, and by the time they had reached the bookstore, she wanted to scream. The fluorescent lights were glaring, and the people in the bookstore seemed to crowd her. Laura's breath was coming in quick, hard bursts.

"I'll be right back, Nana," Laura said.

"Mmhmm, okay honey."

*Thank God, somewhere quieter.*

A wooden table toward the back of the store was piled high with discount books. Laura saw a book bathed in black flowers. Flipping through the pages, she felt her racing heart slow and the heat emanating from her body dissipated. It was a book of quotes from someone named Mary Wollstonecraft. Her radical feminist politics littered the pages. Laura smiled.

*Sammy will like this.*

Laura couldn't imagine Sammy ever taking orders from anyone, let alone a man. Laura's mind cleared as she made her way back to Nana and Maddy, book in hand.

After the bookstore, Nana decided to cross the length of the mall once more to find new winter jackets for Laura and Maddy. They wound through the claustrophobic crowd, back to the other end of the mall with the cheaper stores. Nana didn't have enough money to buy two coats from the stores where Laura used to shop. Laura also suspected that Nana would have to lie to her father about how much money she spent on the coats, so better to keep them cheap so that a smaller amount was missing.

They walked into the department store, its giant red letters gleaming above the entrance. One of the letters was unlit, so instead of the sign reading Crimmons, it read Crimmos.

*That looks really pathetic, why don't they just get someone to fix the bulb?*

Tinny holiday music hummed in the background, and there was a distinct smell of plastic in the air. Laura led the way to the Girls' section where there were rows and rows of jackets, most of which looked like silver, shiny marshmallows.

*These are going to make me look like a giant snowman.*

"Maddy, dear, do you like this jacket?" Nana held up a puffy blue jacket covered with pink flowers.

Maddy quickly turned to Laura and made a gagging motion.

She turned back to Nana.

"Um, I don't know," she said. "Maybe this one?" She held up a dark navy blue and red jacket. It had a lightning bolt on the sleeve.

"But that looks like boys' clothes," Nana said.

Maddy shrugged. "I like it," she said simply.

Nana huffed a little and muttered under her breath something about dressing like a lady. Maddy rolled her eyes and took the red and blue jacket over to a mirror to try it on.

"And Laura, what jacket do you like, honey?" Nana asked.

Laura still hadn't found one that was appealing.

"Um…" she muttered.

"Hey, Laura!" She heard a familiar voice call from across the lines of clothing. Sammy's high ponytail bobbed toward her, weaving through the racks.

"I thought I heard you," Sammy said, smiling. "My mom's over on the other side looking for some clothes for me. What are you doing here? Oh, look at these jackets!"

Sammy grabbed a large silver jacket with a green lining that looked like an unopened can of peas. Laura suppressed the urge to groan and reached for one that was barely tolerable.

"I guess I'll try this one on," Laura said to Nana, holding a puffy pink jacket with tiny gold stars.

"Is this your grandma?" Sammy asked.

Before Laura could reply, she had walked over to Nana, holding out her hand like the mayor. Nana smiled and shook the outstretched hand, looking at Laura.

"Nana, this is my friend Sammy from school. Sammy, this is Nana."

"Nice to meet you," Sammy said grandly.

At that moment, Maddy ran over with her blue jacket on.

"Cool coat," Sammy exclaimed. "Are you Maddy?"

Maddy looked back at Sammy suspiciously. "Yes," she replied. "And who are you?"

"Maddy, this is Sammy, my friend from school."

"Hey," Maddy said, and then turned to Nana. "Can I get this one, please?"

"Okay, fine," replied Nana.

"Laura, are you getting that one?" Nana asked, pointing to the jacket Laura was holding.

"Yeah, I guess so," Laura sighed.

*I don't want to be a bitch, but these jackets are so ugly. Poor Nana, I feel bad.*

She imagined walking into school on Monday, encapsulated in pink puff, and a small shudder ran through her.

Nana nodded. "Maddy, come with me, we'll go check out."

"We're almost finished shopping, and I was going to head over to Jane's for a bit." Sammy made a small, almost imperceptible motion with her hand as if she were smoking her fingers.

Laura laughed a little.

"Okay, I'll tell Nana that I'll head out with you and be home later. I'm sure she won't care," Laura said.

A tiny thrill of excitement tingled in her spine. A year ago she would have never imagined that she would sneak away from a shopping trip to smoke weed, but a year ago she would have been on this trip with her mom.

*My outside world has changed so much in the last year, why wouldn't my inside world change as well?*

"Nana," Laura called. "I'm going to head out with Sammy. We're going to a friend's house, but I'll be back for dinner."

"I was going to take you girls to the food court for ice cream. Does Sammy want to come?" Nana asked.

*She's trying, she truly is.*

She hesitated.

"No, thanks though. I'll see you back home later."

Nana looked sad for a moment, but then the cloud passed, and she shrugged. "Okay, be careful and have fun," she said.

Laura turned away from Maddy and Nana and she followed Sammy through the racks and past the decorated mannequins. Sammy paused for a moment to jokingly lift the skirt of one of the mannequins.

"Nope, nothing there," she said, laughing.

They found the exit for the store, and Sammy pushed the door open. The blast of December frost bit at their cheeks. The cold air felt good on her hot face and neck, and she relished it for a moment. They began to walk down the sidewalk toward the coast, to Jane's house.

*That house is so dreary and decrepit, maybe I should have stayed with Nana. Oh well, Sammy's with me so it will be fun no matter what.*

"Your Nana is nice."

"Yeah, she is."

"Why don't you talk about them much?"

"Who, my family?"

"Yeah, I don't get it," Sammy paused. "You don't have anything to be ashamed of with me. My dad is a complete screw-up. It can't be worse than that."

"My dad is a screw-up, too," Laura said. She squinted her eyes a little at the brightness of the sun and didn't meet Sammy's eyes.

"What do you mean?" Sammy asked.

"I don't know…he drinks a lot. He gets really mean and mad. It's gotten worse since my mom died. I try to stay away from him, but sometimes it seems like all he wants is to fight with me," Laura said. It was the first time she had been able to say those words aloud, and it felt good to hear them.

Sammy looked at her. "I know what you mean. My dad used to do the same thing. He never apologized for anything. Once, he took his baseball bat and swung it at me. It missed my head because I ducked. My mom was watching the whole thing. That was the night we left the house."

"I thought he left you?" Laura said.

"Not really, we had to escape him. My mom needed to get a restraining order and we stayed in a shelter for a few weeks until my grandma could wire money to get us out here. I don't think I'll ever see my dad again," she said. "It's weird because even though he did that, and he hurt my mom a lot, I still love him. Isn't that crazy?" Sammy had her hands in her pockets and she was talking very fast. Laura thought she might be trying not to cry.

"I love my dad, too, even when I hate him," Laura said.

Sammy shook her head.

"What is that? Biological programming? Survival instinct?"

"Who knows? All I know is that no matter how much I try, I can't stay mad or hateful toward him all of the time. And believe me, I want to. But, I can't."

The streets were getting narrower, and the sun was beginning its slow, early descent. They passed by men standing in alleys, leaning against brick walls, smoking cigarettes, following them with their eyes. One of them called Sammy "sweetheart," and Sammy replied with a passionate "fuck you."

Children were riding their bikes in the street, their breath appearing in foggy, gray puffs. These roads seemed to garner less attention from the town, as if they lay in a forgotten pile, like ratty, torn clothes. The sidewalks were less even, and potholes dotted the pavement. Garbage was tossed in yards and on the street. The dark blue garbage bins stood nearly empty.

"Is it okay that we're walking over here?" Laura asked.

"Yeah, it's safe. I walk here a lot, and nothing's ever happened," Sammy said.

Tendrils of fear circled Laura's mind. Shadowy figures seemed to lurk behind overgrown bushes and around telephone poles.

"Here it is," Sammy said.

*Finally.*

Laura looked up at the house. The last of the weak winter sun sinking behind the roof made the front yard look even more gloomy and dismal. Dried up matted grass flanked a cracked stone pathway leading up to a set of wooden stairs with planks missing. As they walked toward the house, the smell of propane lingered in the air, and goosebumps rose on her arms. It looked like a horror film set. Sammy knocked on the door a few times. There was no answer for what seemed like an impossibly long time. There were sounds of horns honking and children playing in the distance. A dull wind blew through Laura's hair.

"Good house for Halloween," Sammy said under her breath.

The door began to creak open, and Jane appeared. Her dark hair looked even more unkempt than usual, and she peered up at them from behind thick, black-rimmed glasses. It was hard to see, but purple circles rimmed her eyes as if she hadn't slept well in ages.

*Okay, maybe I shouldn't have come here.*

"Hey," Jane said from inside the house. "Laura, I didn't know that you were coming." She said this in a tone that sounded accusatory. Sammy seemed completely unaware of Jane's subtle hostility.

"Oh yeah, I saw Laura at the mall, thought she might want to join us," Sammy said.

Jane shrugged. She beckoned them further into the house, and Laura felt slightly sick seeing the house's insides. The outside had looked broken down, but the inside looked like it hadn't been cleaned in centuries. A few lamps dimly lit the old, scratched wood floors, and she could see dust in the corners of the walls. Long cobwebs stretched in dark corners, and the fireplace was filled with ash and gave off a sooty smell.

Jane led them up the creaky stairs. The bedroom on the left of the corridor had piles of clothes on a mattress and a bare lightbulb hanging from the ceiling, flickering slightly. Posters of women lined the walls, placed methodically in rows, some in bikinis and others with their breasts bared. Their eyes seemed to follow Laura as she walked by. Her stomach turned again.

Jane's room wasn't much better. She, too, had a lone mattress in the center of her bedroom. The sheet on it was a dull greenish-gray and the smell of old socks lingered in the air. The walls were covered with Jane's art: dark, shadowy, cloaked figures drawn in pencil or charcoal, many standing on precipices and looking down over cliffs or up at the immense night sky, shaded black with streaky, erased dots that must be stars. Jane was a good artist, but her work frightened Laura.

*I would be mortified if I lived in a place like this. The duplex is bad enough. Maybe that's why Jane was so rude earlier.*

Jane flicked on a small lamp sitting on a green wooden dresser. The lamp looked like it belonged in a nursery. It was pink and had a faded teddy bear standing on the base, smiling kindly. Laura stared at it for a little too long.

Jane's eyes were on her, and she snapped her head around. Her face looked threatening as if she were daring her to say something, but Laura remained silent and sat down on the edge of the mattress with Sammy.

Sammy began talking loudly and excitedly about a funny story from English class while Jane retrieved the bag of weed and a small glass bowl from the top drawer of her dresser. The bowl had rainbows painted on it, and they seemed to gleam a little in the faint sunlight streaming through the blinds on the window. Jane packed the bowl carefully. She grabbed her lighter, nodding along with Sammy, lit the bowl, and inhaled deeply. She passed the bowl to Sammy.

"Want to do something fun?" Jane said with a wicked grin.

*What the hell is she talking about?*

Sammy passed Laura the bowl as Jane left the room for a moment. There were rustling noises and the sound of a drawer creaking. Laura breathed in the acidic smoke and some of her jangled nerves began to ease.

"What's that?" Sammy asked as Jane walked back into her bedroom, holding a wooden board with numbers, letters, and a dial.

*Shit, I know what that is.*

"It's a Ouija Board," Jane announced, holding it up so that they could see it clearly. "I got it for Christmas last year."

"That's a weird gift," Sammy said.

"Not really," said Jane coldly. "It helps me with my art."

"What do you do with it?" Sammy asked.

"Contact dead people," Jane replied with an evil grin.

The pieces of the puzzle of Jane were beginning to come together.

"No, thank you," Sammy said. "My mom said she saw a ghost once, when she was little, right after her grandma died. She didn't sleep in her bed for two months after. I do not want to see one."

"Me neither," said Laura.

The room was starting to feel too hot, even though it had been icy cold when they arrived.

*I've got to get out of here.*

Laura began to rise from the mattress.

"But Laura, I brought this out for you," Jane said. Her eyes blazed in the sunset, and for a moment it looked like they were on fire.

"What do you mean?" Laura asked.

"For your mom," Jane said.

"My mom?" Laura looked over at Sammy. Sammy was looking down at the mattress, toying with a hole in the corner. "You told her?"

Sammy looked up, her cheeks red, "She already knew, Laura. She asked. Kids at school talk about it sometimes, you know." Sammy looked down again.

Laura's heart was pounding in her ears. Tears were rising in her throat, but she didn't want to reveal her weakness by crying.

*Of course, I know that everyone knows about my mom, but I didn't expect it would be a topic of conversation between my best friend and a girl I hate.*

Jane shrugged, and there was a glint behind her eyes.

"I thought you might want to contact her, that's all. Sorry," she said in a way that was altogether unapologetic.

Jane threw the board down on the mattress. Sammy was still looking away. The bowl was sitting on the wooden floor with a weak line of smoke rising from it.

There was so much inside of Laura that wanted to spew forth. She fought the urge to yell in both of their faces, to spit, stomp, and scream. The rage was blinding. Her hands curled into tight fists to keep from clawing at both of them.

*I'd love to grab Jane's black hair and throw her into that stupid Ouija Board.*

Laura was frozen, though, and she stared at them, panting slightly. Then she grabbed her coat and ran down the dingy stairs and out the front door, slamming it behind her.

The streets were black and lit only by lamplight and car headlights. Even the houses seemed dark, their owners not home from work quite yet. It seemed she was running through a dense forest, filled with thick pine trees that stretched tall into the blackness. There were lurkers still prowling in the shadows.

*I dare any of you to catch me right now.*

Her house appeared like a beacon of light in the clearing of the vast forest. Heaving open the front door, she stood for a moment, trying to catch her breath. Dizziness swirled, and through her kaleidoscope vision, the outlines of Maddy and Nana sitting and playing cards appeared. Full shopping bags sat in the entryway.

*Good, Dad's working the night shift.*

Nana might have said something to her, but she was somewhere beyond the forest, and Laura couldn't reach her. Then, she was lying on her bed in pitch black, sobbing uncontrollably. In between heaving breaths, a shadowy outline that looked like Nana appeared in the doorway and the words, "She needed a good cry," floated in on tendrils of light pouring in from the hallway, then heavy footsteps as Nana walked back into the shadows.

*Laura's mother piled her and Maddy into the car the day before Christmas Eve, their breath creating rings of smoke in the air. Even the laziest neighbors had found time to trim their tree and put up their lights, and they loved driving through the neighborhoods, looking at the decorated houses. Her mother had put on their mittens and placed thermoses of hot chocolate in their hands. It took a few minutes for the car to warm up, so the girls giggled and puffed on the cold windows and drew shapes in the fog their breath made. The car sputtered a little as Laura's mother placed it in drive, and it began to descend the steep driveway. Laura and Maddy sipped carefully from the thermoses, enjoying the sugary chocolate that coated their lips. The car wound through the neighboring streets, and they oohed and ahhed at some houses while playing harsh critic for others.*

*"How could they think blue lights would look nice?" Laura's mother would say, with false airs.*

*"A light-up snowman? Tacky!" Laura would comment.*

*There was always one house that no one could critique, however.*

*The Pullman's home stood at the end of the cul-de-sac. It had an iron gate that, if you peeked through at the right angle, revealed an ornate white door and large windows cut into the brick walls. Laura could see tiny white lights glimmering against the brick, and the white door had a large, fresh, green wreath on it, strung with hundreds of small white bulbs. Candles glowed in each window, and in the giant picture window, a tree stood, swathed with golden ribbon, decorated with fruit frosted with silver sparkles. An angel sat on top, intricate and designed with great detail, a benevolent smile playing on her lips.*

*They didn't know the Pullmans and had never seen them coming or going from their home, until one year when Laura had seen a beautiful young woman appear in the window.*

*She was holding a steaming mug in one hand and a small boy in the other arm. They were smiling and pointing at the angel, and then they stepped away, disappearing into the glowing warmth of their house. Laura always wondered about the story of that mother, who she was, and how she came to live in such a glorious house. Laura wondered if she was happy. She certainly appeared so, and who wouldn't be, surrounded by that castle, insulated from the world by money and beauty.*

*That year, Laura's mother drove them home in silence, and when they stepped inside their small house, she went directly to the shower and stayed there for a long time.*

The holidays had swept through with an icy chill uncharacteristic for December in Connecticut. Nana watched the news report nightly. The temperatures had dropped below zero, so the reporters were bundled in scarves, hats, and mittens. A brisk wind kicked up snow, swirling it around their faces, and coated their coverings with powdery white.

Laura was relieved that the frigid tundra outdoors put absolutely no pressure on her to see Sammy for a while. Nana wouldn't let Laura walk the slick sidewalks in such freezing temperatures. Once or twice the phone rang for Laura, Sammy on the other end, wanting to get together or see a movie. Nana had made a realistic excuse for Laura each time, blaming the weather or her father, as Laura shook her head no vigorously, alerting Nana not to let even a hint drop that she might be home. Nana didn't press Laura for information on what had happened, and for that, she was grateful.

Even her father was home very little, either at work or out at the bar. When he was home, he spent most of his time sleeping soundly, like a great hibernating bear, only rising to eat or use the bathroom, before retreating back to his burrow. The holidays passed in a quiet way, and Laura felt something like peace.

Christmas morning was actually comfortable. Nana made sticky buns, covered with white icing, matching the white-topped houses that could be seen through the frosty windows. Laura's father was home, and although he snuck some bourbon into his coffee, he was more alert than he had been in a long time. Nana remarked that he had always loved Christmas as a boy, often waiting up to see Santa until far past midnight, and then sleeping late while his brothers cried to open their presents. Her father had laughed at this story, and for a brief moment, the lines etched around his eyes seemed to lighten.

At two o'clock, Nana brought out a large Christmas ham. Maddy made hot chocolate topped with marshmallows for everyone, and they enjoyed this strange combination while the radio hummed holiday tunes in the background. As night fell, the small tabletop tree twinkled with tiny colored lights, and Maddy lay on the floor coloring in her new superhero book. Laura's father had flipped through a few channels until he settled on watching *It's a Wonderful Life*. He settled back in his chair and half closed his eyes. Occasionally, Laura would glance at her father or Nana, who was also watching the movie quietly, but intently. Once, her father wiped his face, and his cheek glinted in the light of the Christmas bulbs. Nana sat very still, with her hands folded in her lap, until the very end when George, dirty and exhausted, picked up his daughter with a tear-streaked face. Nana's shoulders began to shudder slightly.

The light of the television glared in the darkness.

*What would it be like if I had never been born?*

A sea of blankness met her; it was hard for her to fathom.

*What would it be like if Mom had never been born? Of course, I wouldn't be here, and neither would Maddy. I have no idea where Dad would be. Probably living under a bridge. I also wouldn't have to be the girl whose mom had died. But, Mom made so much joy. The way she saw the world was so different but made so much sense. Is it better to live a short life with such intensity and cause so much pain in its wake, or never live at all?*

Laura peered into the shadows beyond the television.

*Is death really the worst thing, as so many people make it out to be? Jane makes it into some spectacle. I think it's something different, but I don't know what exactly.*

Laura tucked herself into bed that Christmas night, the sound of Maddy's breathing echoing in the dark room, and drifted off into a deep sleep full of angels' wings and her mother's face.

Winter Break ended abruptly, and with it, the Christmas chill lifted. Laura walked to the school bus in the morning amidst a spring-like thaw, the once frosted trees dripping water into grey ponds beneath their branches, and the snow-coated sidewalks and houses now returned to their usual ugliness. The white snow had hidden the defects in the small, ramshackle homes, glazing them like gingerbread houses. It had made Laura yearn less for her old neighborhood.

When she arrived at the bus stop, Sammy was there already. Laura had been dreading this moment for days before school reconvened. Sammy knew that she was avoiding her.

*Maybe the whole Ouija Board incident wasn't completely Sammy's fault, but still.*

Sammy flashed her eyes over at Laura several times as they waited for the bus. Laura tried to look down at the ground the whole time, appearing very interested in the watery brown run-off from the dirty snow flowing into the storm drain. She could feel Sammy's eyes like two weights.

The bus pulled up, louder than ever, spraying brown sandy sludge from the road.

*Oh great, first day back after break, and my tights are covered with mud.*

Laura boarded the bus and slid into a bench that was torn apart, save for some duct tape attempting to patch together the ripped vinyl. White fluff popped out from around the tape like bits of Santa's beard.

With a thump that shook the already loose bench, Sammy sat down beside Laura, a small smile on her face. Laura turned to look at her and then turned back to the window.

"Guess you survived Y2K?" Sammy said jokingly.

Laura didn't respond.

"Hey," Sammy said, a bit harshly. Sammy's smile was gone.

"This is bullshit," Sammy said.

It looked like her eyes were filled with tears. Laura hugged her backpack tightly on her lap and hid behind a curtain of hair, looking down at the dirty floor.

"I didn't do anything wrong, Laura, and you know it," Sammy said loudly.

"I don't want to talk about it here," Laura hissed.

"Oh, give it up Laura. No one cares. No one cares about you, no one is paying attention. Why do you always care so much about what everyone else thinks? Why are you always hiding from everyone?"

Laura leaned her head back on the seat and closed her eyes. Her cheeks burned red.

*It's true. I do care. I'm embarrassed all the time, ashamed, fearful of being found out for being poor, orphaned, alone.*

Laura turned around and faced Sammy. The noise of the bus was a low roar and she knew that no one could hear them.

"I care because I have nothing else," Laura said. "Everything I had is gone."

Her hands were white and red, gripping her backpack like a life preserver. She struggled to breathe and she was annoyed to find that tears were rising up into her eyes.

An arm reached around her shoulders and drew her in close. Laura could smell a faint waft of smoke emanate from Sammy's breath and her striped black sweater reeked of cigarettes.

"I'm sorry," Sammy said, quietly.

"I know," Laura replied, and she turned away from the window and put her head against Sammy's shoulder, exhausted.

<h1 style="text-align:center">April 2000</h1>

Orange light shone from the gym windows like wolf eyes flashing in the dark as Laura and Sammy walked up to the heavy red double doors propped open with school desks. Flyers for the fundraiser were held down by a stack of textbooks, and Tara, another freshman, smiled up at them, her braces glinting in the lamplight. Music thudded the concrete sidewalk. Laura normally preferred the quiet melody of acoustic over the howl of electric guitars. But, she had promised Sammy that she would come along and the warm spring night beckoned.

"Hi!" Tara said. "Donation box is over here, and here is a pamphlet with tonight's bands listed."

She handed them out cheerfully, talking loudly over the music. Laura took the pamphlet and placed her $5 in the donation box. Sammy grabbed the pamphlet then grabbed Laura's hand and pulled her, smiling, into the open gym.

"You have to donate to get in," Laura said.

"I don't have any money, I spent my last $5 on this." She opened the flap of her denim jacket to reveal a flask tucked inside her tight waistband. "Besides, it's just Tara, She doesn't care."

*That's true, but you still shouldn't have done it.*

However, the glint of the flask called to her and whispered in her ear a song of excitement. She could almost taste the clear burn of the alcohol on her tongue.

"Okay, okay," Laura said.

"Oh, so you're happy I didn't donate now, are you?"

Laura rolled her eyes and smiled.

"Come on," she said and took a few steps ahead. Sammy trailed just behind.

Laura, nodding at a few people she knew, made a line for the back corner of the gym where they would go unnoticed. Everyone seemed to have a film of dew on their body, and the smell of old cigarettes, weed and stale alcohol lingered like a dense cloud just above the crowd. There were chaperones, but they were likely in their own corner, probably sharing a flask as well. The two youngest teachers in the school were always at these things, Ms. Lapin and Mr. Rice, but they were probably off in an empty classroom together, or at least that was the rumor.

The fog of body heat was oppressive, and then suddenly it lifted and fresh, cool air hit her face. It was even a little quieter in this corner. The music still hammered, but it had the quality of listening to a dentist's drill while drifting through laughing gas. Close yet far away at the same time.

Sammy hopped up on a windowsill and pushed the glass open further to let more of the cool spring night air float into the humid gym. She handed Laura the silver flask and then lit a cigarette. The glow of the lighter made her face seem almost ghostly, and Laura's mind flashed unwittingly to a night with her mother and Maddy, years ago, when Maddy was just a toddler.

*"Mom, can I have another s'more?"*

*"No, sweetheart, you've already had three. Come here and sit next to Maddy. One of the best parts of a campout is telling ghost stories."*

*They had built a soft pink blanket fort in the dining room, propped up with wooden chairs and kept in place with heavy books. Her mother had held a flashlight up to her face, casting dark shadows along her forehead and cheekbones, toning down some of her gentle beauty and creating a ghoulish image that was both frightening and familiar. Laura's spine tingled as her mother spoke in a deep, ghostly voice telling stories that, looking back, were probably pretty lame, but at the time they were mesmerizing.*

*Her mother was so close to her, sitting on the floor, the softness of her worn night robe rubbing her cheek as she snuggled her head into her lap, looking up into the shadow of her mother's face.*

The memory sprung to life in front of her eyes so vividly that she grabbed the flask and sipped the slightly warm, fiery liquid. In the face of alcohol, the memory retreated, back into a small box in the corner of Laura's mind. The fuzzy sensation of vodka swimming through her bloodstream lulled her senses.

The music paused for a few moments.

"The band is switching," Sammy said, flicking her cigarette out of the open window. "Come on," she said. "Fly by Night is my favorite."

This time Sammy led the way through the crowd up to the very front of the stage.

"Sasha Turner is the lead singer for them," Sammy explained. "She's the only girl here tonight onstage, and she has an amazing voice." Sammy drew out the word amazing and kind of flapped her eyes back in her head.

After they had made up, Laura had given Sammy her Christmas present. Sometimes, Sammy would quote it on the bus to school, when she would go off on some diatribe about feminist history and how women should have the same opportunities as men. Laura thought the obsession might have to do with Sammy's mother who was always trying to get Sammy to wear dresses and, as Sammy put it, be a "girl." When Sammy said "girl," the tone in her voice dropped to utter disgust.

Sammy had a weird relationship with boys. She would flirt with them mercilessly, sometimes to the point of discomfort for the boy and for any onlookers. Sammy always had to be in control, and would never show weakness or vulnerability in any way. She liked to watch boys squirm in her presence; a secret smile would turn up the corners of her lips, though only Laura would know that this wasn't part of the flirtatious act. It was a smile of satisfaction, the way a cat would grin when it caught a mouse. Laura would stand by quietly, laughing along at times, but more often feeling vastly uncomfortable by the display.

Sammy didn't ask Laura to hang out with Jane anymore.

*Thank God.*

But, when they had hung out, Laura noticed that they occasionally brushed hands and smiled at each other in a way that seemed more than friendly.

*I don't care if Sammy likes girls, I care that Jane's a bitch.*

Sammy never said anything about it, though, and Laura wasn't sure how to bring it up, or if she should even ask.

The band had set up and began playing. Sammy was right, Sasha was a great singer. Her hair was jet black. She wore tall black boots and stomped around the stage. The wave of students behind them cheered and sang along. The dueling noise rocked Laura's body and her head swam with the intensity.

"Give me some more of the flask," Laura yelled in Sammy's ear above the music.

She slipped open the top and poured some more of the fire down her throat as the music throbbed. Even her heartbeat seemed to keep rhythm.

*Someone's watching me.*

She felt the heavy presence of eyes. Laura glanced around, quickly stuffing the flask in her jeans pocket.

*Crap, did one of the chaperones come back and now they're actually trying to do their job? Wait a second…*

Joey Trafalgo, the bass player for Sasha's band, was gazing at her and smiling. He was sixteen, two years older than her. Laura had known of him since middle school, even though they had never had an actual conversation. His reputation always preceded him, and many of the stories of teenage mischief that spread like wildfire through the students always seemed to end with him. Sometimes she would pass him in the hallway as they switched classes, and occasionally their eyes would happen to meet. He had the type of eyes that looked blank, like the person behind them had hidden themself so deep inside that they were afraid to be seen. He was the only person she had ever seen in her life with such blankness, it both scared and intrigued her. Through the haze of body sweat and the alcohol in her veins, Laura felt pulled into his stare like a tornado. It was almost impossible to look away.

Laura wasn't sure what was different that night that drew her to Joey. Remembering that night many times over the next year, it was like reading a favorite book a second time, delicious to savor but nothing like the intensity of that first night.

"He keeps staring at you," Sammy said, grinning at Laura, halfway through the band's second set.

"Like I can't see," Laura said, self-consciously swinging her long brown hair to the side and smiling.

"I thought he was still with Jenny Brooks," Sammy replied. "But knowing Joey, that won't matter to him too much."

Laura shrugged. Most of the boys in school thought of her as a wallflower. It wasn't until just recently that they had seemed to begin to notice her. Laura had never kissed anyone, let alone had sex, and when a boy did try to flirt with her, she usually just turned red and laughed until he gave up.

This was awkward but preferable.

Sometimes the attention was fun, but other times the flirting felt grossly simple and juvenile. She knew that she was pretty. Everyone told her. But she didn't want to be flirted with just to boost the ego of a fourteen year old boy. Laura yearned to be truly loved, and so far, no one had even tried.

After the band played their set, Joey hopped off the stage and walked straight over to Laura and Sammy.

"Hey," he said, looking at Laura.

"Hey," said Laura, with Sammy silent beside her, grinning and squeezing her arm too hard.

"I'm just going to go grab something to drink," Sammy said, motioning vaguely to a table with a giant punch bowl in a far corner.

She squeezed Laura's arm again and walked away, swallowed by the hot darkness of the gym, leaving Laura alone with Joey.

Laura nodded and turned back to Joey.

"You played really well."

"Oh, thanks," he said. "Hey, want to go outside where it's cooler? The stage lights and the set really heated me up."

Laura could see that his smooth cheeks were flushed and sweat beaded on the upper lip of his boyish mouth. He had his hands in his pockets with his thumbs sticking out, and his shoulders shrugged up to his ears.

"Sure," Laura replied.

He led her out of the double doors and they walked on the sidewalk to the other side of the school. Some boys whooped and called out to Joey. His dark brown hair was wet with sweat and it glistened in the light from the lampposts. Every so often he would wave to a friend, but mostly they walked in a silence that was surprisingly comfortable. The night wrapped its arms around her, and she floated as if in a dream. Some small urge to be touched blossomed inside of her belly.

*Maybe Joey will hold my hand.*

"Over here, no one will see us," he said and hopped up on the long hood of his beat up '87 Chrysler LeBaron.

The brown paint had been scratched, and it looked like he had tried to paint over it himself. Laura tried to look away from the marks so as to not embarrass him. In the last two years, she had learned what it felt like to be poor. The discomfort of that vulnerability had lit a new sense of compassion in her. Being poor was not easily hidden, nor escaped from. Laura found that it followed her around like a lost puppy dog, and no matter how much she tried to shove it away, it kept reappearing at her doorstep.

Laura climbed up beside him on the hood of the Chrysler and looked out into the emptiness of the night. The football field stretched like long shadowy hands. Black evergreens dotted the edge.

*It's probably pretty late, I forgot to check the time. Oh well, no one is going to look for me. Nana's likely fast asleep and dad's probably out cold in an alcohol-induced stupor by now.*

The respite from his drinking had not lasted, and as February rounded its corner, he had taken a deep nosedive back into his drug of choice.

"You're in Mr. Pete's 7th period Spanish class, right?"

"Yeah," Laura replied.

"I'm in his 2nd period. He's a real asshole, right? Whenever I see him waiting outside his classroom, I picture myself taking my Spanish textbook and just chucking it at him."

Laura and Joey laughed a little at his mildly violent fantasy.

"Want some?"

Joey reached into his pocket for a joint and held it out for Laura. The alcohol's dreaminess had receded, and she was in the mood for something softer.

"Sure."

She placed the joint in her mouth and he held the lighter up to it. With a spark, smoke began to pour from its tip. As he pulled his hands away, his fingers lightly brushed her chin, where the scars from her father had left pale indents. Laura breathed in the grassy smoke and the smell was like earth and flowers after heavy rain. Her shoulders dropped a little, and she passed the joint over to Joey. He was quiet for a long time, which she liked. So often boys her age talked about nothing for far too long. He seemed wiser, more aware of the world.

"You live by the water, don't you?" Joey said after a while.

"Yeah, on Peaceful Street."

"I know," he replied. "I live on the opposite side of that road. Sometimes I drive by you while you're waiting for the bus."

Laura laughed, "You should stop and give me a lift!"

"I will from now on," Joey replied grinning. "It's real shitty, you know, living down there. You tell people, 'Oh I live by the water.' If they're not from around here, they picture you in this big house with a huge deck looking out on the ocean, waking up to the sound of waves every morning. No way, I tell them. No way. Here the water is just a dump. In fact, it smells like garbage most days, don't you think?" He shook his head and passed her the joint.

"It does. Every time I go down to the beach, I find needles, used condoms, and trash. It's really sad, actually." She sucked in the smoke.

"Yeah," he sighed. "Our world is dying and no one seems to give a fuck."

Laura leaned back on her elbows and gazed up at the stars. They seemed to grow brighter and brighter until they filled her vision like spotlights. Anything beyond them, even Joey, was hard to see. His voice sounded very far away. Perhaps he was actually across the football field, she didn't know. Then she felt a hand on hers, warm and soft, eager, and the brush of soft skin on her lips. Joey had kissed her for the very first time.

## June 2000

A fine mist sprayed as Joey and Laura walked out of school at the end of the day, holding hands. The gray sky above seemed to sink in around them, hiding them with its gentle fog. Everyone in school knew that they were together, but Laura didn't like to put it on display. Some couples would lean against the lockers entwined for the three minutes between classes, but Joey and Laura were not like that. It wasn't until they walked to Joey's car in the afternoon that they would touch for the first time all day.

Joey had taken to driving Laura to and from school each day. In the mornings at 6:45 sharp, he would sound one honk outside of her duplex. Sometimes her father was awake, sitting at the kitchen table, with cold coffee and a cigarette. He would turn to her with cold eyes, call her a slut, and Laura would look at him for a moment as if he were made from air. Then, she would turn and run out the door, slamming it behind her. Most days though, he was asleep in his bed, bottles littered across the floor and his world spun into oblivion. It all seemed to bother her less since she wasn't home very often, anyway.

Joey liked to drink, too, but not like her father. When Joey was drunk, he was soft and sweet. He would transform into a poet, spouting soulful lines that Laura would sometimes copy down into her notebook to turn into lyrics with her guitar later on.

In the mornings on the way to school, Joey would often open a small flask filled with vodka, and they would take turns sipping from its cold rim. When they pulled into the parking lot, Joey would pull out a bottle of fluorescent blue mouthwash, to disguise the alcohol on their breath.

Sometimes, Joey would pick up Sammy from her house and take her to school. She never drank with them. Not that she didn't like to drink, weed was just preferable, and it was too stressful to try to get high or drunk before class. Sammy wouldn't ever admit it, but she was smarter than Laura, and she took pride in getting good grades, especially in math.

Laura, on the other hand, began to care less and less about the things she used to care so much about, such as getting good grades and staying out of trouble. It was freeing not to care. Her world with Joey and Sammy edged everything else out. Joey was a rock. He seemed to know everything, and he carried himself with such confidence and strength. Laura held onto this in him because she couldn't find it in herself.

Laura didn't follow Sammy to the park anymore after school. Sammy usually went off with Jane. Laura would often catch a glimpse of them walking through the trees, still naked without their leaves, and in the bareness, Sammy's voice would echo.

Part of Laura missed those afternoons, but a silent understanding had arisen between them. Sammy could be friends with Jane, and Laura could be friends with Sammy, but Laura and Jane were not to be in each other's presence again. Besides, Joey always had an empty house in the afternoon. His mother was rarely home. She was a waitress and a bartender, and she left the house for work in the afternoon. His father had left when he was only one, supposedly with his secretary, but Laura thought that sounded too cliche and wondered if she would ever hear the real story. Joey kept his family pain close to his chest, as did she. Together, they found ways to escape the hurt that lived in each of them.

The grey day encircled them as Joey held open the door of the LeBaron for Laura. Laura carefully side-stepped the missing plank of the porch steps as Joey opened the front door. Inside, the house smelled of mildew and damp. It was reminiscent of the duplex. Joey led her to his bedroom, up a narrow wooden staircase and toward the back of the house. The smell of mildew was milder up here, but it was replaced with an odor of stale smoke that hung in the air. This wasn't unpleasant to Laura. It reminded her of the smell of Joey's tee-shirt when she would lay her head against his chest and he would wrap his arms around her. They spent a lot of their time like that, clinging to each other.

56

Laura sat down on the edge of his twin bed and looked up at the band posters surrounding his bed.

"How do you sleep with so many faces staring at you all night?" she asked.

Joey smiled, "I like the company," he said. "Sometimes I talk to them, and if I've had enough of this," he signaled to his flask, "I could swear they were talking back."

Laura hugged her knees up to her chest.

"And what do they say?"

"Mostly they just quote their songs back to me," he laughed. "It actually helps, I'm able to see their lyrics in a new way. It helps me write my own stuff."

He put his flask to his lips and drank slowly. Laura enjoyed watching him do this. She liked looking at his hand, encircling the flask. While the rest of his body was somewhat short and a little stocky, his fingers were thin and long.

*Maybe that's why he's such a good bass player.*

"Can you show me some of your songs?" She asked.

"Here, first let me get you something," Joey said. His fingers worked carefully, delicately, rolling the joint. "Have some while I grab the songs."

She inhaled the smoke deeply and felt an instant sense of lightheadedness and relaxation overtake her. Joey handed her a pile of papers, mostly bent and crumpled. Pencil scribbles were etched across the pages, and it appeared that staying in the faint blue lines of the paper hadn't mattered to him. Laura glanced over the pages and saw that many of the songs were filled with rage. She looked up at him.

He seemed to read her look intuitively.

"It's an outlet," he said. "I can be angry on that page so I don't get angry and get in trouble in my real life."

"That makes sense," she said.

*Wish Dad would do something like that.*

He looked at her for a moment. "Here, put these down," he said as he crossed the small room to sit beside her.

Taking the songs gently from Laura's hands, he placed them on the floor beside the bed. Then, he pulled her body against his and they laid down on the thin, worn mattress. Laura felt her entire body relax, and he stroked the tips of her fingers. They hadn't had sex, yet. She wasn't sure she was ready. Joey knew this, and would only go just as far as she liked. For now, that meant simply touching and sometimes pressing their bodies together. It ignited a fire, but Laura wasn't sure what to do with it.

At around 7:00, they would leave the soft warmth and glow of his bed and the fog of alcohol and weed that surrounded them.

*I hate leaving. I know I'll see him tomorrow, but it's hard to say goodbye.*

Laura hated going back to the darkness of her home, waiting to see him, trying to figure out what to do with that fire inside of her. Late at night, once Maddy was breathing rhythmically and the house was silent, Laura would think of Joey and touch herself. She would lay on her stomach and press deeply into her hands, building pressure until a burst of stars floated in front of her eyes, and her body would shudder with deep drumbeats of pleasure. This calmed her immensely, and she would fall asleep quickly afterward.

# July 2000

The summer flowed like water. Days passed like bursts of color, each one brighter than the next. Time stood still and then sped up so that sometimes it seemed as if life were a bullet train, and other times it felt as slow as a flower waiting to blossom.

Laura was a still point in the center of a shifting and evolving landscape painting. Sometimes, she found herself lying in Joey's bed looking up at the soft purple sky with pinprick stars. Other times, the scene shifted, and she was sitting on the floor of Sammy's room, laughing into a smoke filled void about something she later could not recall. Life moved pleasurably in this way, although Laura began to feel removed as if her life were a movie screen she was watching.

Laura took care to hide the smell of smoke on her clothes and the vodka on her breath from her family, and so far, it had seemed to work. Once or twice, Nana had given her a second look after she returned home from Joey's or Sammy's house, but she had never said anything. Her father was home less than ever, and she was thankful to see him only in passing, often in the morning when he dressed, and made his way to work, sloppier than ever. His attitude toward her had shifted from hatred to disgust to complete detachment. When they did make eye contact, it seemed that he was staring through her, and only occasionally did he grunt a few words of greeting, as if startled from a deep, internal sleep that he was loath to wake from.

Most summer evenings, Joey would drive Laura and Sammy to his friend

Tim's house, to watch their band practice. Tim lived on the other side of town, the side that Laura had moved from. He had a large white house with a two-car garage and a long paved driveway with a basketball hoop. Tim's mom would often cook dinner and serve it on giant platters on a folding table in the garage. Towers of spaghetti with homemade sauce and plates of garlic bread would appear, as if by magic, halfway through band practice. Laura and Sammy would sit on the old yellow couch in the corner of the garage, balance their plates on their laps, and tap along to the songs. It was too loud to talk, but sometimes they would sneak sips of vodka from the flasks they brought along. Laura would pull hers from deep inside her purse. It was nestled in the inside zipped pocket where she kept it, in case her bag ever tipped over and spilled out, or Maddy thought to reach into it.

*Wow, he plays so well, it seems so natural for him. I love watching the way his fingers move on the bass. I love him, I think I do at least. Does he love me, too? I wonder what I would say if he said it first.*

Laura loved many things about Joey: his laugh, his songs, the way he stood with his arm around her, protective but not possessive. She loved watching him play on stage. He stood, slightly hunched over the bass guitar, his fingers moving deftly along the strings and a look of concentration on his face that made his lips pout a bit.

*I know what it means to love. I love Mom, Maddy, Nana. I love Dad, even while I hate him. But, what is falling in love?*

Even with the constant stream of love stories playing in her head from an early age, from Cinderella to Snow White, and more, she couldn't be sure that this was love. Laura's heart was dancing on a precipice, but her mind seemed to pull her back so that she wouldn't tip over the edge. Deep love was entwined with deep loss for Laura, and she wasn't sure she could withstand more heartbreak in her life.

After the band had put away their instruments and the plates of food were gone, Joey wrapped his arm around Laura's shoulder and they walked out to his car with Sammy beside them. Darkness was settling in on their part of the world. Laura had always loved summer nights, how long it took for the sky to turn black, and the shades of color that appeared in the darkening. Winter nights were like flipped switches, someone walking into a bright room and turning out the light. They always felt slightly eerie.

Standing here, under the streaky twilight, the alcohol buzzed warmly in her mind.

"Do you think you could drop me off at Jane's?" Sammy asked.

Joey nodded as he slid into the driver's seat of his car. Laura suppressed a shudder.

"Thanks," Sammy replied as the motor roared to life.

A slight smell of exhaust arose and then disappeared as Joey cranked open the window and threw his hand out to wave goodbye to his friends. Tim called goodbye, illuminated by the glow of his large house. Sammy lit her cigarette in the back seat, the tip a firework of orange. They made their way through the suburban streets, houses lined up neatly, many with meticulously cut and kept lawns and gardens. Summer was in full bloom, and rows of hydrangeas, rose bushes, and daylilies sprouted from the seas of green. The moon looked like a thin fingernail etched into the blackening sky. Laura saw the beautiful surroundings and felt a pang in her chest. Although her home had never been large or fancy, it was small, neat, and comfortable. Living on this side of town, she supposed she had always felt rich by association.

*I wonder if Joey and Sammy ever feel jealous of these houses and the lives of the people that live in them. Although it's harder to have something and lose it than never have it at all.*

The wide suburban streets narrowed as the car wound its way through the shadows. Laura knew that Jane's house was lurking at the end of the dark road they had just turned on. She slid down further in her seat as if to hide herself from Jane and her haunted house. Sammy and Joey had been chatting about his band and music, although Laura had barely noticed until Joey put the car in park and silence fell.

"You can both come in, you know," Sammy said awkwardly.

"I know, thanks, Sammy, it's okay," Laura replied.

Sammy shrugged and opened the car door.

"Bye, Joey. Talk to you tomorrow, Laura."

Sammy walked up the broken-down pathway and knocked on the crumbling door. Joey stayed until he saw Sammy go inside.

*He's a gentleman like that.*

Laura caught a glimpse of Jane standing in her dark doorway, cast in shadows, wraith-like, a shadow herself. Rumors had been swirling that Jane was getting into harder drugs. Laura had asked Sammy about this once, and Sammy had shrugged it off.

"I don't make her choices," Sammy had said.

"I'm not saying you make her choices, I'm just asking what yours are," Laura had replied, frustrated at Sammy's nonchalance.

Sammy had looked out of the window, blankness coating her face.

"Look, I know we both drink and smoke, but I don't want you doing the scarier stuff."

Sammy had rolled her eyes, "Oh Laura, don't get all D.A.R.E. on me now."

The conversation had been futile. Sammy wouldn't admit to using harder drugs, even though Laura suspected that she was. Sammy seemed far away somewhere, a place she couldn't reach and would never want to reach. Watching Sammy walk through Jane's front door cemented a loneliness in Laura that had been brewing since the holidays. Joey helped to fill some of the void, but she missed Sammy in a way that was intense and full of longing, even when she saw her every day. Sammy was hiding a part of herself in that dark place Jane lived.

The door closed behind Sammy, and Joey drove away. It was now fully dark out, the purple tinged light had disappeared from the sky, and there was a bite of chill in the air, even though it was humid. Joey's car slithered through the streets. It was quiet. Laura liked that he didn't blast music. He loved music as she did, but he had said he never understood the need to turn it up so loud. It was much more enjoyable to listen to it so that you could actually hear it, rather than just blaring noise.

Joey had been a little drunk during band practice, but he seemed calm and clear now. He placed his hand on Laura's lap as he steered through the streets of lamp-lit houses, each with their private stories walled off from the world by wood and glass. He was driving them down to the town beach, which sat on the coast but felt like the edge of the world. They always climbed to one spot in particular. It was up a paved path, and then a short climb up a grassy hill, to a cliff that looked out over the Sound. Small waves crashed against the piles of rocks that had lain there forever, smoothed over time by the constant beating drum of water. Laura loved this spot. The sound of the waves soothed her, and she always felt cleaner somehow after being there.

Joey parked his car in the dimly lit lot and opened the door for Laura. He held her hand as they walked. It had been silent on the car ride since Sammy had gotten out, but a nice kind of silence.

"Don't let Sammy and Jane bother you," he said, finally cracking open the silence. Laura looked up at him.

*Why is he saying that? He doesn't know about Jane and the Ouija Board or anything.*

"What do you mean?" she said.

The rhythmic splash of waves echoed through the darkness. Up ahead, the black silhouettes of trees and rocks stood solidly in their place. The chill from earlier had dissipated slightly, and she felt calmer.

Joey shrugged. "You always seem so uncomfortable whenever Sammy talks about Jane or sees Jane. Maybe you don't realize it, but I can tell."

He paused for a moment to take his flask from the pocket of his shorts, and he took a deep drink.

"Not too much," Laura laughed. "You do have to drive me home later."

Joey smiled, "I know, I know. Just a little to take the edge off. It is getting chilly out here."

He shivered a little and his smile darkened as he looked out at the water. They were getting closer to their spot on the cliff, and the waves were getting louder.

"All those rumors about Sammy and Jane…" he trailed off. "Some of my buddies have said…well, I've heard they're doing some pretty hard shit."

Laura's heart sank.

"Look, I like Sammy, and if you want to be friends with her, I'm not going to stop you."

They had reached the bench and sat down, sliding close to each other.

"Sammy was there for me last year when no one else was," Laura replied. She pulled her arms around herself, clasping her elbows, and bowed her head a little.

Joey held his hands up. "I get it," he said. "That's like Tim. Even though he lives in a fucking palace, he's been my friend since we were little kids."

Laura nodded.

Joey turned toward Laura. His delicate fingers reached for her chin, and he drew it up gently to look into his eyes. Laura saw stars sparkling and lights shimmering on the water out of the corner of her eye. Joey's eyes appeared like black pools of water.

"You're a good girl. Don't forget that. It's who you are."

He pulled her face closer to his, and then kissed her eyebrows and then her lips, and she melted into him, soft, small, and childlike.

*Am I?*

The night settled in around them.


The new school year was approaching quickly, and time seemed to speed up from the lazy, colorful flow of summer. Laura knew fall was coming by the way the light fell. Soft light and shadows at six o'clock meant the cold season wasn't far away.

Laura, standing at the kitchen counter, began to chop carrots and prick bruised potatoes for roasting. Nana had bought them from the bin at the grocery store where they threw the near-rotting produce. She pulled chicken from the refrigerator and placed it on a sheet pan with the other vegetables.

It was an easy dinner and one that her mother had always loved to make. After roasting for a bit, the chicken would flavor the vegetables and the ingredients would meld in harmony like a song. Laura realized the shape of her grief had changed over the last year, from pointed and spiky to round and soft. Her sadness and memories lived in a space that was untouchable by the outside world.

At that moment, the red door heaved open and a burst of cool air followed her father into the small, glowing duplex.

*God, it seems like it's been years since I've seen him.*

Lines of fatigue had appeared on his face that hadn't been there before. He closed the door behind him and stood for a moment, facing the door. Then he took off his shoes and placed his wallet and keys down on the small table that stood at the entryway. Laura tried to read his body language for a clue to his mood. Nana was still in her bedroom and Maddy was in their room. The storm cloud on the horizon was now right overhead. She wanted to escape, to run and hide in the back of the house, or run out the door, but she knew that might anger him. Besides, dinner needed to be made.

*Just try to stay calm. Get dinner on the table.*

He walked over to her with slow, steady steps.

*He hasn't been drinking, at least.*

The oven began to beep, and Laura opened the door, releasing a pulsing wave of heat that blew her hair slightly. She pulled the roasted chicken and vegetables from the oven and placed it on the stovetop. Her father watched her in silence, his hands in his pockets. Laura avoided eye contact and tried to shrink her body to make it as small as possible.

She began to set the table, carefully laying out white paper napkins and the utensils her mother had used since she was a girl.

*Not too long ago, Mom held the same fork and knife, brought it to her lips, maybe smiled and laughed while holding it.*

It was an odd, vulnerable thought to have with her father standing there, staring at her, but it floated to the top of her mind nonetheless.

Laura's father folded his arms against his chest. He hadn't changed out of his security guard uniform yet, and his bulky, lurking presence felt a bit like being watched by a cop. He made small, almost imperceptible movements with his fingers and neck. This shift from stillness to movement signaled his mind working, chewing over the words that he was about to say.

"So," her father said.

The one word cut a channel in the silence and, like water, more words began to pour from him.

"This boyfriend of yours. I've been thinking about him." He paused as if waiting for a reply.

*Oh no, why is he talking about Joey?*

Laura couldn't think of anything to say, so she simply nodded. A knot of tension was forming between her eyebrows.

"Well, I think it's time we met him, don't you?"

*This might be an innocent statement for any other parent to make. If Sammy had a boyfriend and her mother wanted to meet him, a statement like that might be friendly, welcoming.*

However, the words cascading from her father's mouth felt like drops of poison pouring from a bottle. They were ominous, threatening. "Slut" was an arrow he had drawn back in his bow and aimed at her, now a barb stuck in her back.

*No, I really don't think it's time for you to meet Joey.*

The thought made her want to vomit. There was no way to refuse this request, though. His questioning tone was daring her to deny him. Laura continued to look down at the plates and nodded a little.

"I think a nice, family dinner is in order," her father said.

Laura looked up now. Her father was smiling a little, in a way that showed his exposed teeth but did not extend up to his eyes. It looked wolfish and hungry. She could barely suppress a shiver.

"I'll ask him to come over tomorrow," she replied in a small voice.

Her father clapped his hands together and bared all of his teeth.

"Great," he exclaimed, and he whisked past her to his bedroom to change out of his uniform.

Laura stood frozen, staring down at the plates, lost.


Time passed too quickly the next day. Nana went to the store to buy some more groceries to make roast beef and potatoes for the family dinner. Maddy was playing outside with the children who lived on the other side of the duplex. They were quite a bit younger than her, but they occupied her most days of the summer. Laura sat in her darkened bedroom, shades drawn against the dying summer light. She had barely been able to eat the night before, and in the morning, she had only just kept down some buttered toast.

After last night's dinner, she had walked to Joey's house through the darkening streets. Her father had left right after the meal to go to his favorite pub. She had brushed her long hair several times and then slipped on a soft, white sweater to keep out the damp chill that fell at night, the saltwater droplets from the sound cast far from their home with the wind that always seemed to pick up in late summer. Laura had called to Nana that she was going out to visit Joey, and Nana had given her a kiss on her cheek and told her to have fun. Maddy was in some other world filled with superheroes and villains.

*A tidier world. Good always seems to win in those stories.*

Maddy had found comfort in imagined lands and men and women who could save the day ever since their mother had died, and Laura didn't want to pull her out from her haven. It seemed to help her cope.

The streets were quiet and dimly lit as Laura walked the few blocks to Joey's house. It sat slightly apart from the other houses, and, although it was smaller, it was neater than Laura's house. Joey's mother, even though she never appeared to be home very much, kept two small window boxes with yellow flowers, and Joey cut the grass and weeded the pathway every Saturday for her. Windchimes hung from the small porch. Joey's mother loved to collect them, and on breezy days, the music sounded both joyful and melancholy, depending on which chime was brushed by the wind at each moment.

Joey hadn't known Laura was coming, but he answered the door quickly and with a smile.

"Come in," he said, motioning for her to step over the threshold.

"No, I really can't stay too long," Laura said. "I just had to ask you something."

"What is it?" Joey asked quizzically.

He stepped onto the porch and drew Laura onto the small wooden bench sitting underneath a flower box.

Laura sighed.

*I know Joey won't mind coming over. He's wanted to come for a while and I keep brushing him off.*

"My dad wants to meet you. Tomorrow. For dinner at our house," Laura said, nearly stumbling over the words.

"Okay, great," Joey said, shrugging. "I'll figure out something better than this to wear." He pointed down at his grey sweatpants and holey t-shirt.

Laura laughed a little and then said, "Just so you know," she paused for a breath, "My dad, I never know who he's going to be every day. Sometimes he's okay or just leaves us alone. Other times he's angry and mean. It depends on whether he's been drinking, or just whatever his mood is. I'm saying all of this because I don't know who he's going to be tomorrow."

"I really like you, Laura. I don't care about your dad."

Laura breathed a sigh of relief.

"Okay," Laura said, resting her head on Joey's shoulder.

They sat like that for a while, until Laura realized an hour had passed.

"What time is it?" Laura's body jolted upright.

Joey peered down at his watch. "Almost nine, do you want me to walk you home?"

"No," Laura shook her head. "That's okay."

"See you tomorrow," he had said with a wink.

She just smiled and walked back to the duplex, feeling a little lighter.

The lightness hadn't lasted. The next morning a dark fog of anxiety weighed itself across her chest like a heavy blanket. It was smothering, and it only intensified as the day passed. At times, Laura had to sit down to gasp for air.

Nana was in the kitchen all afternoon prepping the roast and pricking potatoes.

"A true roast beef gravy is one of the most delicious things on Earth," Nana said.

She was teaching Laura how to scrape the pan for drippings, add flour, a little milk, and broth.

"And you get the creamiest gravy known to man."

Nana loved to cook and bake. Sometimes she was too tired to do much of either, but when she did, the result was delicious. It was comforting to sit in the kitchen and watch her stir the spoon around the great, grease-speckled roasting pan. The day seemed to make much more sense with Nana in the kitchen like the old days.

At 5 o'clock the late summer shadows were growing long, and the front door knob clicked. Fear returned like an old friend. Laura rushed from the kitchen to her bedroom and closed the door.

*Dad's home, ugh. I really don't want to see him until I absolutely have to. He better be sober.*

Footsteps thudded through the hallway, and the bedroom door closed. Relief flooded her body, and she opened her closet to decide which dress to wear for dinner.

*"Red looks beautiful on you, my love," Laura's mother said. "Here, wear this one." Her soft hands reached into the back of Laura's closet, past the play clothes, and pulled out a bright red dress with a plaid skirt.*

*"Look, you can wear this bow, and it will match perfectly." She held up a red bow that had sparkling silver beads dangling from the ends.*

*Laura's mother dressed her, carefully zipping the back of the dress to avoid catching Laura's skin, smoothed out the plaid skirt, and rolled her tights on. She brushed Laura's hair with the copper brush that belonged to her own mother, sighing with just a hint of sadness as she remembered her.*

*Then, she looked at Laura and said, "You look like a princess."*

*Laura felt like a princess. She paraded through the house in her patent leather shoes that reflected the tip of her nose when she bent to look at them. The rain started just as it was time to leave for dinner. Laura's father wrapped her in a raincoat and carried her out to the car so that she didn't ruin her shoes.*

*Laura sat in the back of the station wagon, watching the droplets pour down the windows. The gray day was turning to night, and streetlights bounced their reflected, yellow light into the windshield, creating a mirage that looked almost like sunlight.*

*At dinner, Laura ordered a Shirley Temple with extra cherries, and she filled up on bread from the bread basket, even though her mother kept warning her not to. She wanted to sit on her mother's lap while they were waiting for their meal, it was taking so long, and she was too old for the crayons and paper menu they had given her, but too young to be able to sit patiently and enjoy the grown-ups' conversation. Her mother had scolded her slightly for fidgeting and told Laura to stay in her seat. Her belly was too round for Laura to fit in her lap and, besides, she should act like a young lady at dinner. Laura pouted a little and then rested her chin on her hand, gazing at the other diners around her.*

*The food arrived, but Laura could feel her mother growing tense. Short, tight lines had appeared around her eyes, and a frown twitched at her lips. Laura looked over at her father, who was ordering another glass of something brown. She looked back at her mother. Her shoulders had risen and her upper back had curved slightly as if she were trying to protect herself from something.*

*"Happy anniversary, sweetheart," her father said.*

*But his words came out funny like his tongue had tied a knot in his mouth and his words were tripping over it to get out. Laura laughed a little, but her mother shot her a stern glance, eyes ablaze, and Laura bent her head and resumed eating her chicken.*

*Her father stood up, mumbled something about using the bathroom, and then turned to Laura. He paused for a moment, and it seemed like he was trying to say something, but the words were stuck. His hand was resting funny on his belt, and Laura wanted to laugh again, but this time the laughter inside of her felt anxious and uncomfortable.*

*Crouching down, he looked into her eyes with a glassy stare, and then his body heaved forward. It heaved again, and this time brown liquid sprayed from his mouth all over Laura's beautiful red dress and her shiny patent leather shoes. She froze as the smell of sour vomit rose around her head like a fog and she heard herself saying over and over again,*

*"My shoes."*

*Her mother lunged at her and pulled her upright as her father fell down on the floor panting and writhing and laughing almost maniacally. The other diners in the restaurant had fallen still and silent in total shock as a few servers flocked around Laura and her mother, offering wet towels and looks of condolence. Another male waiter had heaved her father around his shoulders and was walking him out the front door to the car.*

*Opening the car door, the waiter shoved her father's mass into the backseat. Sweating and grunting a little, the waiter positioned him in the backseat on his side. Laura had to sit in the front passenger seat while her mother got behind the wheel.*

*Her mother was screaming and crying and her father was moaning in the backseat. Then there was a hot shower to rid herself of the stinking vomit. Her dress and shoes were thrown directly into a scalding rinse cycle in the washing machine and her mother had used so much soap that the small plastic cap overflowed with sticky liquid.*

*Tucked into bed, far past her bedtime, smelling of soap, Laura finally spoke.*

*"Is Daddy going to be okay?"*

*"Daddy will be fine, my love."*

*She looked out the window at the full moonlight that shone through, casting soft white shadows on the walls.*

*In a voice barely above a whisper, she continued, "I'm not so sure about us."*

Dinner was hot and delicious. Laura tried to focus on that in the heavy silence that had poured over them like rich gravy after the awkward introductions. Joey and her father had shaken hands with quick nods and without direct eye contact. Laura had led Joey over to the chenille couch and Nana, smiling warmly, had brought them both Coca-Colas with extra ice.

Her father had lingered by the front door, his large bulk casting a shadow across the tiny living room. He was still wearing his security guard uniform from the day shift and hadn't bothered to change.

*Why is he still wearing that?*

Nana set the table in the kitchen while Maddy sat in the chair across from them, reading a comic book and twirling a strand of hair over and over. At one point, Joey tried to reach over for Laura's hand. It brushed against hers, moist with sweat, and she brushed him away, shaking her head slightly.

*Dad's going to kill both of us if he sees him touch me.*

It was best if a thick void remained between them.

Every so often, her father would clear his throat behind them and pace a little. Sometimes he would call out to Nana to ask when dinner would be on the table, but mostly he just stood like a monolith behind the couch.

"Dinner's ready!" called Nana, shattering the tense silence.

Relief flooded Laura. Maddy jumped off her chair, oblivious, and rushed to the dinner table.

"Mmm, roast beef," she exclaimed, and dove in.

Laura's father sat down at the head of the table, heaving his bulk into the small chair. The classic cartoons of clowns pouring out of a toy car flashed in Laura's brain.

*Oh my God, don't laugh, don't laugh.*

Joey cleared his throat.

"So, Mr. Thompson, you work at Meyers Park as the security guard, Laura tells me?" He sounded very polite and formal.

*Impressive.*

Her father glanced up from the precise job of folding his napkin and placing it on his lap then looked down again, creasing the folds.

"Yes, been there twenty five years."

"Do you like the job?"

Her father shrugged.

"It's a job," he said, cutting off an opening for further conversation. Silence resumed.

Nana, smiling, tried to revive the conversation by asking Joey about school, his car, his family.

*Thank you, Nana.*

After dinner, Nana and Laura stood to clear the dishes.

"I'm going to take a walk outside, want to join?" Laura's father asked Joey.

His eyes darted to Laura for a moment and then he looked back at the hulking man in front of him. Laura saw him swallow hard.

"Sure."

The clock ticked audibly after the front door banged shut. Laura's father had poured a glass of whiskey for himself, no ice, and taken the rest of the bottle with him for the walk.

*Fuck.*

Many minutes later, Laura was patting the dishes dry, and the front door still hadn't opened again. Sometimes it looked like the light from her father's cigarette moved past the window. It glowed ferociously. However, there were no raised voices echoing in through the cracks in the house.

*That's a good thing.*

Nana watched Laura.

"Your father is a good man, at his heart, Laura. He truly cares about you."

*Yeah right.*

Laura just nodded and looked down at the plate that was now completely dry. She continued to circle it with the dish towel.

"Any father would want to meet their daughter's boyfriend."

*That's true, but Dad isn't any father.*

He vacillated between complete neglect of her and her sister, and totalitarianism, running his household like a country trapped under a brutal dictator. Laura didn't know which was worse. Both were lonely.

The door began to creak open and Laura's head whipped around. The shadow of her father was long in the lamplight and seemed to spread through the living room into the hallway. He stepped inside an empty glass in one hand, and an empty bottle in the other.

"Where's Joey?" Nana asked.

Her father didn't answer. He looked down at the carpet.

"This rug really needs to be vacuumed," he said, his words slurring slightly.

"Where's Joey?" Laura repeated.

He looked up now, and the look in his eyes made Laura feel sick.

"Oh, Joey, he had to leave." The wolfish grin had returned. "Something came up," he sneered.

Laura's head swam and the kitchen, warm from the oven heat, turned upside down in front of her eyes. She slammed the plate she had been drying down on the counter.

"What did you say? What did you do?"

Normally, fear kept her tongue still, but not this time. Her voice rose, she roared. Her chest was vibrating with rage. It felt like power.

Surprise flashed across her father's eyes. The women in his life didn't stand up to him, and this was unexpected. He paused.

Maddy, who had gone to her room right after dinner, peeked her head around the corner, and then retreated back into the bedroom, closing the door quickly behind her.

Laura felt a hand on her shoulder. Nana. She was breathing deeply and whispering. Laura knew that she was praying.

Thick, stifling tears began to rise in Laura's throat.

*Don't cry, that will only show weakness.*

Laura couldn't help it. She buried her face in Nana's shoulder. The fabric of her blouse was soft and smelled comforting. Nana wrapped her arms around her and kissed the top of her head. Her father stood as still as a statue. He began to speak, but it sounded more like a growl.

"I don't want to see him around here again. You are not to see him again."

Laura turned around. Her face was red and wet with tears and snot. She looked like a three year old having a tantrum, but for the first time, she didn't care.

*Mom's not here to protect me now, I have to protect myself.*

"What did he do that was so wrong?" she cried.

Her father stepped forward and bent down so that he was face to face with Laura. His eyes were bloodshot, and his breath was hot with anger and whiskey.

"It wasn't him," he laughed with malice. "It's you. I saw the way you looked at him. The way you walked in front of him. You're a whore," he growled. "You make me sick."

He spat these words in her face and saliva sprayed her lips.

"Jacob, don't," Laura glanced at Nana.

She was cowering. There was terror in her eyes. For the first time, Laura realized how afraid Nana was of her son. Exhaustion filled Laura. She was tired. Tired of the strands of fear that connected her with her mother and grandmother, all pressed down by the thumb of one man.

Laura unhooked her shoulders from her ears.

"I am not a whore, and I am not afraid of you."

Her bag was hanging on a hook in the entryway. Laura stepped past her father, grabbed her bag, opened the door, and in one swift movement, stepped out into the dark night.

*I'll look back once.*

Her father was standing in the doorway, illuminated by the light of the broken lamp that no one had ever fixed. He was yelling curses at her and stomping his feet, but for some reason, he didn't follow her. The security guard uniform that had looked so intimidating just hours before now looked ridiculous.

*He's basically a mall cop.*

Laura began to laugh a little, and then a little more until she could barely control herself. Her mouth was open wide to the stars, and her belly hurt from gulping the air as she laughed and laughed, and the night seemed to laugh with her.

# March 1994

*The car was dark and the streets were black. Laura couldn't tell where the darkness began and ended. There was something on her mind. Maybe the seed was planted long ago, left to germinate in the earthy warmth beneath the surface of her conscious thoughts. Today, it sprouted a tiny bud of green and then began to grow very quickly from its roots. Now, the seed blossomed into a flower of curiosity that Laura had been inspecting since she overheard the whispered conversation earlier this morning at recess. They were standing in line, waiting to be escorted back into school. The blacktop was cold on this grey March day, and Laura was standing patiently, playing with the zipper of her raincoat absentmindedly when she heard the conversation begin behind her.*

*"You saw them?" Sadie asked Christina.*

*Christina giggled. Laura could almost hear her blushing.*

*"What did it look like?" asked Rebecca.*

*"Well, there was a lot of skin and they were sort of bumping up and down," Christina had hissed.*

*"Weird," said Sadie.*

*The conversation trailed off into more giggles and whispers as they began to walk into the school, and Laura hadn't been able to make out the rest of the words, even as she tried to lag behind.*

*Sometimes her parents' door was locked, which was odd. Why did they need to lock themselves away? What if something happened and they were stuck on the other side of that door?*

*Laura knew the word "sex." It was sometimes whispered on the playground or in the*

74

hallways, as had happened today. It was something grown up and secret, and that made her insatiably curious. Her own body hinted at what sex might be--when she was tired or sad, she would press into her hands and it would calm and relax her. Maybe grownups did that with each other? It seemed logical. Being a grownup probably felt scary all the time. No wonder parents do that.

The radio played a tune that was blurred by the sound of the rain. Maddy slept soundly in her baby seat next to her. They were almost home. Laura felt her heart start to beat, and she could feel the words sitting in her throat. She coughed a little, hoping to open the trap door to let them out.

"Mom," she started.

"Yes, honey?"

"I know what sex is."

There was a pause. Laura could almost hear the mechanisms of her mother's mind working quickly and efficiently to spit out the perfect response.

"Oh? Well, what do you think it is?"

"It's when two people take off their clothes, hug each other a lot, and jump up and down."

Breath was exhaled, a sigh that sounded like relief.

"Okay, yes." Pause. "Why don't we talk about it later tonight when I'm putting you to bed."

"Okay," Laura said quietly.

Well, at least it was partly confirmed. Christina wasn't lying.

Later that night, after Maddy had cried a little and settled to sleep in her crib, Laura had a glass of warm milk and put on her fleece pajamas against the damp chill of the rain. She sat in the folds of her bed and leaned up against her mother's warm body. A small pile of books sat in front of them. Her mother picked up one of the books and began to flip through it.

There was a fat little man with a drooping mustache, hanging belly, and a small flap of skin, which Laura realized must be his penis, hanging beneath the circle of his stomach. His wife looked exactly the same as her husband, except that she had curly hair, rounded breasts, and a small swath of hair beneath her round belly.

Laura's mother began to read through the book, explaining everything matter-of-factly. She didn't appear to be embarrassed or uncomfortable. Laura thought she sounded like her science teacher explaining the steps the class would take to complete the science experiment.

"And then," she said, "a baby is made."

"So you've had sex, Mom?"

Her eyes flickered for a moment. "Well, yes," she said. "But, only after I was married."

Laura thought about this for a moment. "Does it hurt?"

"Not really, not in the ways you think it would. Giving birth does, but I'll tell you more about that when you're older," she smiled.

Laura leaned against her mother, looking out the window at the flecks of rain illuminated against the glass.

"Well, I think it's gross."

Laura's mother laughed and kissed her, nestling her face into her soft hair.

"You'll think of it differently when you're older and you love someone. It will just feel right."

"Maybe." Laura yawned and snuggled down into the covers. "Good night, Mom. I love you."

"Good night, Laura. I love you, too."

# July 2000

Joey's bed was warm. He lay beside her, asleep, not snoring, but breathing deeply and heavily. It was a calming noise for Laura, who couldn't sleep. A slick of wetness was still sitting between her legs.

A few hours earlier, she knocked on his door. He opened it and looked at her for a moment.

"Should you be here?" he asked.

"No."

"Come in."

Wordlessly, they climbed the stairs. Laura's senses were alive. She breathed in the musty, now familiar smell of his little house. The wood railing felt smooth and oily from the years of hands that had held it for steadiness. A dim light bulb swung a little, sensitive to the motion of two pairs of feet.

Joey's bedroom door creaked open, and they walked in, footsteps beating out the same rhythm. There was a small lamp on the nightstand that cast shadows across the walls. Her shadow, usually small and bent over, looked tall and upright.

*If I turn at just the right angle, will my shadow show the thumping of my heart?*

They sat down on the bed together, still in silence. Joey's breath smelled faintly of alcohol, and a half-empty bottle of vodka sat beside the bed, within arm's reach. He seemed steady enough, though. His gentle, long fingers brushed a strand of hair out of her face, and then his fingertips trailed down her neck, touching it ever so slightly until his hand reached inside of her shirt and began to knead and thumb her breast. Laura had pushed this moment off for so long that she didn't realize how much she desired it.

*Are we really doing this?*

The lamplight cast the shadows of their moving bodies on the wall, and Laura watched them as if there were two other people, two strangers entwined in the night. She felt both within and without. More in her body than ever before in her life, and also more disconnected from her body, as if she were watching shadow people do their shadow deeds.

The pleasure was intense, but so was the desire to cry, and it was difficult to understand the dueling sensations. When it was over, Joey flicked off the lamp and darkness descended. Silence still enveloped them; they hadn't spoken a word since she arrived, and that was okay. Laura felt wanted, needed, in a way she never had before, and that feeling was more intoxicating than any sip of vodka that ever burned her throat or puff of smoke she ever inhaled.

# September 2000

The air cooled and the trees shook off their leaves like wet dogs. Laura spent very little time at home. Joey's house was her refuge. After dark, she would creep back into the duplex and leave first thing in the morning at precisely 6:32 when Joey's car would slide down the street to take her to school.

Joey had started attending night school, and after he dropped her off, he would drive over to Craig's Auto Body and fix cars until 3 o'clock. Then, he would pick her up from school and they would drive back to his house for the afternoon and evening.

Joey's house was always empty. His mother was a ghost. She would appear suddenly, say hello while pulling her bleached blonde hair up into a ponytail and strapping on her waitress apron, then evaporate again not to be seen for days.

Joey didn't mind this arrangement. Food from the restaurant was often sitting in the fridge, and they would sit on the couch watching television and eating slightly soggy leftovers. Then, they would walk upstairs and hold each other, sometimes more, until the darkness was so deep, that Laura knew Nana would be upset if she didn't make her way home. Joey would hold her hand tightly and kiss her warmly before she turned and walked down the pathway to the front door, opening the entrance to her cage and shutting it tightly behind her.

Sometimes, Sammy would come over to Joey's house and watch television with them. Sitting on the frayed couch, Sammy would chew loudly and gossip through the reheated fries, spraying small bits of food on herself and anyone foolish enough to sit too close to her. More and more often, she came over high after an afternoon with Jane. Joey and Laura would exchange glances, but he always let her in.

Sammy seemed to be in a hot air balloon, floating through a cloudless sky, rising higher and higher. It was impossible to talk to Sammy about this. Lashing words then pouting was her method of choice for dealing with any sort of conflict, and Laura became afraid to confront her. When they were watching television, Sammy would look blankly out the window, with empty eyes staring out of a paper white face. This frightened Laura, but she didn't know what to do.

As the weather grew chilly, Sammy was slipping away. Trying to hold onto her was like cupping water in her palms. Eventually, it all dripped out through the open cracks and crevices.

# October 1991

*"I didn't want another child," Laura's father's voice roared through the house.*

*In her imagination, it seemed to knock over small objects, pictures and toys, but voices couldn't really do that.*

*Her mother was trying to speak calmly. "I know, Jacob, I know. Please don't upset Laura, Maddy's already crying."*

*Laura was hiding in a corner of the kitchen. From there, she could see her father pacing in a rage through the living room. Every so often, he would appear in her line of vision, and he looked like a monster from her book Where the Wild Things Are. "They roared their terrible roars," echoed in her mind and she squeezed her eyes closed.*

*Maddy was in a small baby basket next to the kitchen table. The plates hadn't been cleared yet, and there were pots and pans left unwashed sitting on the stove. The screaming continued.*

*"How are we going to pay this? How are we going to afford it?" Laura's father was waving a piece of paper in her mother's face.*

*"It's not a big deal, we have the money, Jacob. Maddy needed to see the doctor, her fever wasn't breaking."*

*There was a pause. Laura hoped that it was over. Her mother walked into the kitchen, red-faced and tear-streaked. She held her arms out to Laura. In a flash, Laura saw her father's hands wrap around her mother's neck and chest. He pulled her close to him, hugging her tightly against his body. For a moment, Laura thought this was some sort of strange embrace, maybe an act of remorse. Then, she noticed how tightly her father was clasping her neck and the fear that traced her mother's eyes.*

"Stupid bitch, I bet that baby isn't even mine."

Now, Laura smelled the reek of alcohol and she knew why her father had arrived home later than usual.

"Jacob," her mother whispered evenly, with a false calm so that she didn't frighten her children further. "Jacob, let me go."

Her father released a guttural roar and pulled her mother in closer. Laura could see his wild animal eyes searching for something that wasn't there.

"Please, Jacob. You need help. I'm here for you, I want you to get better."

Her father threw her down with another roar, and she hit the floor hard on her elbow. Her mother winced and held her arm gingerly. A nearly empty bottle of whiskey sat on the entryway table. As her father turned to pick up the bottle and take a long, hard drink, Laura's mother quickly rose, her face a grimace of pain, and in a swift movement, pulled Maddy out of her basket and grabbed Laura's upper arm tightly, so tight fingerprints would be there the next day.

Her father was drinking and talking to himself, swaying a bit on his feet, as her mother rushed the girls down the hallway to the master bedroom. She shut the door and locked it, and then grabbed the chair from her vanity and lodged it under the doorknob so that it would be nearly impossible for her father to break in. Grabbing the phone from the nightstand, Laura's mother sat down on the floor. She swooped Maddy to her breast to calm and soothe her, and she pulled Laura into her wet armpit, holding her arm stiffly so as not to irritate the injured elbow.

Her mother's fingers deftly dialed nine, then one, and then one again. Crashes could be heard from the living room and the sound of volcanic footsteps echoed through the hall. Brutal words spewed from her father's mouth like fire and ash. Laura snuggled in close to her mother and prayed that the door would hold.

"Yes, hello," her mother said, shouting above the banging as her father now threw his body weight against the door.

"I need the police and an ambulance. My husband is sick and very intoxicated, and my children and I are in danger. I believe my arm may be broken."

"Thank you, yes, please be quick."

Outside of the bedroom, the wild thing roared, and Laura closed her eyes. Bits of wood sprayed as the hinges of the door loosened. Her father was screaming, but his words were unintelligible, or maybe Laura had stopped trying to decipher them.

Her mother was a statue, a carved stone Madonna. She sat on the floor with a bared breast and an infant who sucked then cried, sucked then cried. Her older daughter lay against her, eyes closed as if sleeping. The scene almost looked peaceful. Inside, though, a turbulent storm of rage, hatred, and fear brewed thick.

Flashes of blue and red appeared out the window. For a moment, Laura wondered *what she was seeing, and then it dawned on her. Police cars and an ambulance, and even a fire truck, roared in like knights on white horses. Laura bounced onto the bed to look out the window. Her mother had been wise, and lucky. The door had held, thanks to the small, metal vanity chair propped just right.*

*Her father had heard the sirens too, as the banging and screaming halted. Laura remembered the rest of the night in bursts- her father, handcuffed, tripping over himself, with wet pants and vomit on his shirt, being led into a police car. A policewoman taking detailed notes as her mother had to relive every detail, sometimes repeating herself twice. Blankets were given to Laura and the baby, although Laura wondered why given that they were at home and had plenty of blankets and warm clothes. The men with EMT written on their backs set her mother's arm in a navy blue sling. Luckily, it was not broken, but badly sprained, and she would need to work and care for an infant one-armed for the next six weeks.*

*The next day dawned a brilliant blue, the sky unmarred. Laura knew that Nana had picked up her father from jail. He was released on the condition that he would immediately check into a rehabilitation center, and he was not allowed to come home before the treatment program was complete. Six weeks. The time it would take her mother's arm to heal. Laura wondered if her father, after so much hurt and pain and rage, would only take six weeks to heal, too. Some wounds take much longer to scab over, if they ever do at all.*

# December 2000

"Sammy?"

Sammy's head lolled to one side. Her tongue stuck out like a panting dog, but her eyes were blank.

"Jesus Christ, Laura, she needs help."

"Sammy?" Laura cried louder. "Call an ambulance!"

Joey lunged for the phone and quickly dialed 911. Laura could hear him talking to the dispatcher, but it was hard to make out the words. She held Sammy's head to one side, in case she vomited on herself. Laura didn't want her to choke.

Half an hour ago, car lights had shone through the window while Laura and Joey were sitting on the couch watching reruns. It was getting darker earlier now, and neither of them had risen to turn on the lights, so the living room was black except for the blue light of the television. The car lights had startled Laura. She rose to peer through the gauzy drapes. There was a car and a figure, swathed in shadows, carrying a girl who appeared to be unconscious up to the steps of Joey's house.

Laura whipped around. "Joey, come look."

"What is it?"

The doorbell rang. They opened the door and saw Sammy lying on the faux grass welcome mat, her eyes rolled back in her head, the whites gleaming in the car light.

"Oh my God, Sammy?"

Laura reached down and tried to pick her up, but the dead weight was too heavy for her. Joey, who wasn't very tall but had sturdy arms and a strong grip, clasped Sammy underneath her shoulders and pulled her in, balancing her weight against his. The car that deposited her like a piece of garbage, sped off with screeching tires.

Now, Laura could hear the whistle of sirens as she cradled Sammy's head in her arms. Tears were falling. Uniformed men traipsed into Joey's house with a stretcher.

"Is she going to be okay?"

"We're going to do the best we can, Miss," a bearded man with kind eyes replied.

They lifted Sammy's body onto the stretcher, placed an oxygen mask over her face, and began to administer IV fluids. Within just a few minutes the chaos and lights were gone, and Joey and Laura were left looking at each other.

"Are you okay?" Joey asked, touching Laura gently on her shoulder. "We can take my car, go to the hospital, you know."

"I should call her mom," Laura said, moving away from his hand.

She wiped the tears from her face with the back of her hand and went to the phone. Her mother didn't pick up, and Laura stood for a moment staring at the dark room.

*What the fuck do I do now?*

"We should really turn on some lights," she said.

"Are you okay…you're acting really weird," Joey said. "You don't want to follow your friend? See if she's going to live?"

"Joey, I've had enough of hospitals, ambulances, and all of that. You have no idea…" Laura trailed off. Her voice was growing louder.

*I've never been mad at him before, what is going on with me?*

Joey backed away slightly and held his hands up. "Fine, she's your friend." He turned around and walked toward the stairs. "I'm going to bed."

Laura sat down on the couch and sighed deeply.

*I should have followed the ambulance. I should be at the hospital now with Sammy. Her mother doesn't even know where she is, and her stupid friends left her for dead.*

Laura knew very well all of the things she should be doing, but she couldn't bring herself to do any of them. Instead, she sat on the couch, in the dark, until her eyes grew heavy and she fell into a dazed and restless sleep.

Sammy was out of school for over a week. Every time Laura tried to call the house, the phone would ring and ring. No one was ever home. Joey had taken her to the hospital to try to visit Sammy, but the nurse said that only family was allowed in.

Laura began to spend more time at home. Joey hadn't brought up their argument or asked why Laura didn't want to go to the hospital, and Laura didn't push it.

*I could explain everything to him. Tell him about all the dark, hidden secrets that Mom tried to keep so close. Only Nana really knew the truth.*

Talking about it with Joey, though, felt like betraying her mother. She kept those secrets almost her entire adult life, they probably killed her. Laura couldn't bring herself to open that box and piece through it with Joey. As much as she wanted to let him in, there were some places that he, that no one, would ever be allowed to go.

Joey still drove her to and from school. His car would pull up with a roar in front of the school. That was the same, but there was something else, something different between them now. Joey knew she was holding back, keeping a small, dark piece of herself locked away. Another boy may have tried to pry open the tightly shut door, but not Joey. He was gentle, maybe too gentle. It was clear that he wanted her to come to him, and when she didn't, he retreated back into himself like a wounded animal.

*God, I really need to know that Sammy's back home safe. No one seems to know anything.*

Laura would've asked Jane, but she was out of school for a week, too.

*I guess I'll try Sammy's house again.*

She picked up the phone in her bedroom to dial Sammy's number. The phone rang for what seemed an eternity, but Laura hung on. After a few minutes, a small voice answered.

"Hello?"

"Sammy?"

"Yes. Laura?"

"Sammy, oh my God, I'm so happy to hear your voice." Tears began to flood Laura's eyes. She had no idea how much she was holding onto until this moment. Her chest heaved with sobs.

"Whoa there, don't blow a lung. It's not like I died," Sammy laughed weakly.

"You almost did!" Laura exclaimed. "Sorry, I shouldn't have said that."

"No, it's good you did. I need reminding. Maybe it'll keep me from doing more stupid shit," Sammy chuckled grimly.

"What happened?"

"Oh you know, this and that. I guess the coke was laced with something a little stronger. Seems Jane and her brother and some of his friends were trying to play a little joke on me. Real funny." She paused. "Please don't say 'I told you so,' Laura."

"I wasn't going to say that."

"Okay. Sorry I've been avoiding you. I've just been so afraid to hear what I already know."

"I'm your friend, Sammy. I'm not going to make you feel bad."

"Laura?"

"Yeah?"

There was a deep pause.

"Thanks for saving me," Sammy's voice sounded muffled, and Laura realized she was crying.

"Don't make me do it again," Laura said, now crying herself.

"I won't."


Sammy returned to school amidst whispered conversations and penetrating stares, but it didn't seem to bother her too much. Even though the weather was frosty, Sammy and Laura started going to the park more after school, bundled in their tin can winter jackets. Sometimes, Joey would join them. Jane never did. Sammy had banned her from her life, or so she said. Laura sensed a wistfulness whenever Sammy talked about Jane.

"I've lost a lot of people, you know," Sammy said on a chilly December afternoon under the towering oak tree in the far corner of the park. "People I've loved, people I've hated. Sometimes, I just want someone to stay."

"Me too," Laura said.

Sammy never brought weed to the park anymore, and Joey, out of respect, didn't smoke or drink in front of her. Sammy was in a long-term rehabilitation program, but she didn't have to live there.

"Fuck that," was Sammy's response to rehab. "If they made me go live somewhere else, I'd run away."

Laura didn't doubt that. Sammy attended meetings a few afternoons a week, and she had a mentor who was helping her "feel things again."

"What's going on with you and Joey?" Sammy asked.

It was almost Christmas. Her hair was slicked back into a ponytail, and she wore fluffy blue earmuffs that she pushed to one side to hear Laura speak.

"Things are the same, I guess. And different."

"Has he said I love you?"

"Not in so many words. I think he does. He wrote a song for me and played it yesterday. An early Christmas present, he said. It was about a girl. She was sad a lot and liked to stare out of windows. A boy came along and saved her from herself."

"Sounds like he wants to rescue you."

"He does, but he doesn't know what from."

"Are you going to let him?"

"Rescue me? No, I can't. I don't want to. When I saw you that night, left behind, I realized, I can't keep chasing security from other people, always searching for it outside of myself. No one's coming to save me. And if they think they are, like Joey does, well, when he does see me, I mean truly see me, he's going to turn around and leave."

"You think so?"

"I know so."

Sammy stuck her mitten in Laura's cold palm. "You never dress for the weather," she said.

Laura laughed. "I know. Expectations, I guess. I figure I'll get along okay, no matter what the temperature."

Sammy nodded, and they walked together in comfortable silence out of the park, through the darkening streets lit at twilight with glowing Christmas bulbs, then went their separate ways.

# December 25, 2000

They drove for quite some time. The musky smell of weed caked their clothes. Joey had lit up a joint for Laura before the drive, and they were sharing it, passing it back and forth, filling the car with a smoky haze.

"You might need this for where I'm taking you," he said, half smiling.

"Uh-oh, where are you taking me?" Laura had asked.

"You'll see."

The morning had passed uneventfully. Christmas morning, for the first time in her life, was not truly Christmas morning. Laura had given Nana and Maddy their presents and then walked to Joey's house, where she had eaten boxed pancakes and hot chocolate. His mom had left for her boyfriend's house after breakfast, and Joey and Laura had gone upstairs, laid in bed for a while, and then dressed like they were going somewhere until Laura realized they had no place to be.

"A surprise," Joey had said.

"I don't really like surprises," said Laura.

*It's true. No surprise in my life has ever turned out good.*

"You'll see."

Grumpily, Laura had huffed into the car and sat in the passenger seat. The weed was the only saving grace.

"We're here."

Laura had barely paid attention to the roads, she was high and relaxed, letting go of her early irritation. The clouds made funny patterns.

*They're like white mixed with blue. I wonder if there's a name for that color. There should be.*

*Um, what the fuck is that?*

Reality felt like a cold punch in her stomach. In front of her stood her childhood home, the home that she had left only last year, and that now stood, belonging to someone else.

Joey looked at her, grinning. "Merry Christmas."

Laura turned slowly to look at him. Her lips were numb. "Merry Christmas?" she whispered.

Joey's face fell. "What's wrong? I thought you'd like coming back here to visit, especially on Christmas. Good memories and all that."

"How did you even know where to find this place?"

"I talked to your Nana," Joey's voice trailed off as Laura's eyes flared with anger.

"I...I can't believe you brought me back here. Christmas, of all days..."

Joey leaned over to her.

"Hey, hey, I'm sorry, Laura. I thought this would be nice, for you to see your house. I didn't know it would be like this."

Laura pushed herself away from him. "No, you didn't know," she cried. "Because I don't want you to know. I don't want this, any of this."

"Laura, please, you don't tell me anything. I want to love you, but I feel like I don't know you, and I'm just trying."

"You don't want to know me. I don't want to know me."

The tears were falling incessantly, and Laura tried to catch them before they stained her cheeks.

*I hate myself for crying.*

Joey pulled her against him, and Laura was too tired to fight him anymore.

"I do."

She pressed her cheek into his jacket. The wet fabric was scratchy against her face.

*So much time, so much energy, put into protecting myself. Maybe some of it is crumbling. Maybe that isn't the worst thing.*

"Okay, but I can't see the house, not like this. It's too much for me."

"I'm sorry."

They turned around and drove home in silence. Laura sat with her hands folded tightly on her lap, anxious.

*How could I let Joey see me like that?*

When they arrived back at his house, he took her hand and led her upstairs to his bedroom. It was quiet, the Christmas holiday casting a blanket of silence on the normally busy streets. A gentle snow had started to fall.

*It looks so idyllic, like the Norman Rockwell paintings Mom loved. Except in those paintings, families were all together. Now, I'm orphaned, Mom dead, Dad dead in his own way, Maddy deep inside her own cave, and Nana in perpetual fear. And here's Joey, standing in front of me.*

She laid on his bed on top of the soft, red plaid blanket. Joey bent down and kissed her gently on her lips. He began to unwrap her, first undoing the buttons of her sweater, the sweater her mother had bought her two years ago, white and soft with feather fabric that moved with the slightest wind. He undid her bra so that her small breasts stood bare and pointed in the cool room. Joey kissed her neck and then found the button for her pants. Slowly unzipping them, he helped her step out of them, and then he knelt to his knees and pulled down her underwear. Laura had never felt so bare before. Normally, they undressed quickly, excited for the rest of it. Here she stood now, completely naked and still in front of him.

"You're beautiful," he said. His fingers traced the scars on her chin. "I'll undo you," he said.

Laura wasn't sure what that meant, but something tangled inside of her unknotted itself under Joey's gentle fingers.

Now, he pulled her into bed, under the soft covers, and took off his clothes. Entering her, he looked in her eyes, deeply, without blinking, for the few thrusts it took for him to come. They lay together until night fell on the snow covered windows and their empty stomachs commanded them to rise.

*Her mother's belly was round and smooth. When she stepped out of the shower and wrapped her towel around her body, her belly button peeked out, and smiled at Laura.*

*Laura loved to lay her head against the round mountain, full of baby, and feel the tiny kicks and flutters.*

*It was the happiest Laura had ever seen her mother. A soft smile played at her lips throughout the day and she would hum while cooking dinner at night or baking bread on the weekends. Her mother created a sphere of warmth around her and invited only Laura into it, hibernating away from the world with her children.*

*Her father was home very little, and once or twice she saw him stumbling around, but* most of the time he was in his own cave that he had carved out in the basement, thickly strewn with bottles and smelling of old socks and stale beer. They didn't venture down there, they dared not disturb the monster lurking in the depths. Upstairs, in the light and vibrancy of new life, they lived, shuttered and cloistered, happy in their solitude.

# February 2001

*A dream. Laura is standing in a pool of water. She is wearing a white dress and it's wet, clinging to her body. There is light in front of her, but that's all she can see. Light reflected on the water, and light above the water. It is hard to tell where the light ends and the water begins.*

*The air is warm and damp. She reaches her hands down and feels the roundness of her own belly. Music begins to play, and it's otherworldly. It draws on notes and harmonies that she has never heard before but somehow knows. Her belly lurches and vibrates along with the melody.*

*A wave of pressure sweeps over her. Then another one. Contractions are starting.*
*She's not ready.*

*She sinks to her knees, trying to hold the baby in, protecting it. Someone starts to cry, it sounds like a baby's wail.*

*In front of her, emerging from the waves of light, her mother's face appears.*
*"Now you know," she says, and disappears, smiling.*


"You have to tell Joey, you know. He's going to figure it out sooner or later. Isn't he asking why you're not smoking or drinking with him anymore?" Sammy asked.

The day was brightly cold and their corner of the park was deserted. A red cardinal sat in the tree above them, watching them, contemplating something. Laura wasn't sure if the bird was thinking deep thoughts or just wondering where it could find a worm in the frozen ground.

Laura shrugged. "Kind of, but he's trying not to do as much of that stuff either."

"Am I the only one who knows?"

"Yeah, but how long is that going to last?" Laura touched her stomach. Already it was starting to grow. Her thin frame couldn't hide the tiny pouch that extended slightly from her belly.

Sammy sighed. "You know, you could have an abortion."

"I know, I've thought of that, but I don't know if I can. I'm scared, and I feel so guilty when I think about it."

"Laura, if you don't want the baby, what else can you do?"

"Adoption, maybe?"

"I guess, but then you have to go through all the pain of having the baby just to give it up."

"I know."

"It's so not fair that women have to put up with all this. Joey gets to have his happy moment and go on living, and here you are, stuck with a baby inside of you."

Laura put her head in her hands.

"Look, meet me after school tomorrow at the rehab," Sammy said. "Next door is a clinic. I've seen other girls coming in and out of there. We can go in and you can ask questions there. I'll come with you if it will help you feel better."

"Ugh," Laura looked up at the sky, rolling her eyes. "Why did this have to happen to me?"

"It sucks," Sammy nodded. "Facing this tough shit doesn't make it go away, but it makes it easier sometimes." She paused, looking up at the sky.

"What do you think your mom would have said?"

There was a moment's pause between them.

"Sorry I shouldn't have asked that," she said quickly.

"No, it's okay. I've thought about it too, actually. A lot. I think she would have been surprised, and then not surprised. And then she would have told me to make a choice. I guess I would be in the same position I am now."

"Well, meet me tomorrow."

"Yeah, I will."

Laura stood up from the bench. "I'm going to head home," she said. "Want to walk with me?"

"No, I have to think."

"Are you mad at me?"

Laura shook her head. "No, just need some time."

Sammy nodded, "I'll see you tomorrow, Laura." She gave her a quick hug.

Laura walked away, into the light of the setting sun. It shone a bit too brightly. The last few weeks since the pregnancy test she had felt a little nauseous and her head ached. Lights had seemed too bright and sounds too loud. More than anything, Laura wanted to curl into a ball on her bed and stay there under the covers until everything just went away, but she couldn't do that.

Life ticked on. There were tests at school, homework to do, and Joey to see. Joey who had no idea. Joey who kissed her as he always had, who felt happy and smiled when he saw her. That day at the house had meant so much to him. He felt like he actually knew her now. How ironic that now there was a new secret to keep, a new pain buried deep, a pain he had made with her, unknowingly. Laura laughed humorlessly to herself.

*If I were brave, I would have an abortion. If I were brave, I would march home and tell Nana and Dad. I'd call Joey on the phone and tell him. We'd have a real conversation. I'd let that happen.*

*I don't feel brave, though. I feel like a child who's done something wrong and now I need to sweep the evidence of it behind the couch or under a chair. This is too big to sweep away, though. It's going to have to come to light.*

That thought was too big to handle, like trying to imagine the size of the sun or the distance to Mars. Some things her brain just couldn't fathom. She tried to break down the bigness of it all into tiny, fragmented pieces.

*Step one: Go to the clinic.*

*I can do that. I can do step one.*

She breathed.

Laura stood in front of the clinic, housed in a brick building, and her stomach dipped over the edge of a rollercoaster. Sammy was walking toward her, smiling, and waving. Her brightly lit face seemed so out of place. Laura imagined this was where people went to mourn. She turned to wave at Sammy, but she couldn't bring herself to smile back.

"How was your meeting?" Laura asked.

"Oh, you know, same old, same old. They think they know everything about me. Hell, maybe they do. Who knows. Anyway, here we are." Sammy breathed in and looked through the glass doors.

"Here we are," said Laura.

"Are you ready?"

"No."

"I'll go first," Sammy said, and she pushed open the door. Laura followed her inside with her head down.

The clinic was sterile but comfortable. It felt like a doctor's office. Green chairs were lined up along the walls and end tables held piles of neatly stacked magazines. A woman with glasses and brown hair pulled into a bun sat behind a desk.

"Hello," Laura said hesitantly.

The woman looked up from her computer. "Hi, how can I help you today?"

"Um, I was looking to speak with someone privately about um, a pregnancy." The words were hard to get out. Sammy was chewing gum too loudly in her ear.

"Did you say pregnancy?" The woman asked.

"Yes."

"Well, that's what we're here for. What's your name?"

For a moment, Laura had trouble remembering her own name. "L-Laura Thompson," she stuttered.

"You can have a seat, Laura. Please fill out this paperwork, and I'll tell Ms. Foster, our director, that you're here."

"Thank you," said Laura. Sammy snapped her bubblegum.

"Let's go sit over here," said Sammy.

They took a seat in the far corner of the waiting room. Laura began to pick through the paperwork, while Sammy looked through the pile of magazines. The clock ticked.

*I hate the ticking sound of clocks.*

Laura's breath was coming in short bursts when the door creaked open and a woman with a blonde bob and a blue pantsuit stood in the doorway.

"Laura?" she called.

"Yes, that's me," Laura said quietly. She stood and glanced at Sammy once. Sammy gave her a big thumbs up.

"Come with me," said the nicely dressed lady who Laura could only assume was Ms. Foster. They walked down the hallway to the office all the way at the end.

"So, Laura, why are you here?"

The room they were sitting in was supposed to look cozy, not clinical, but it smelled faintly of antiseptic and there were motivational posters on the wall.

*Why are motivational posters so unmotivating?*

"Well, I'm…I'm pregn-," Laura tried to choke out but gave up quickly, cheeks flushed. "And I…I'm not really sure what to do," Laura said to Ms. Foster.

"It's a very brave thing to come here."

Laura shifted a little in her seat. "My best friend made me."

"That's a good friend," Ms. Foster said. Laura nodded, silently. The long sheet of her hair brushed her face.

*I wish I could hide my face. Why can't these things be done over the phone?*

"You know that you have many options. Abortion is one of them. Adoption is another. Keeping the child is, of course, an option as well." She paused.

Laura shook her head. "No, I know that I can't. I have no one, no one who could take care of a baby. I definitely can't."

Ms. Foster nodded. "Then we'll talk about your other two choices." She reached out and patted Laura's hand gently. "I know this is hard, but you have support."

"I'm going to give you a few pamphlets to read, just so you know all of the information. There are lots of rumors out there, and we are dedicated to helping young women like you get the truth about what they can do if they discover they're pregnant."

Ms. Foster handed Laura a few shiny pamphlets that had bullet points and smiling teenagers on them. It seemed too simple.

"Think about all of this, and come back in a few days. I'll be here on Thursday. We can talk about it then."

"Thank you," Laura said. Her mouth was dry and her voice was hoarse.

Ms. Foster stood up and opened the wooden door for Laura. Sammy was sitting in the waiting room, chewing gum and reading a magazine with a picture of a girl with pink hair on the cover. She looked up at Laura.

"How'd it go?"

"Fine."

The receptionist called a cheerful goodbye as Laura and Sammy walked out the glass doors and into the bright daylight.

"So, what are you going to do?" Sammy asked.

"I don't know yet." Laura's head was pounding. She needed water, badly.

"You know, I think you should just have an abortion. Get rid of it. It will be like it never even happened." Sammy shrugged. "You won't even have to tell Joey."

Sammy's words spun in her mind. "Like it never even happened? Sammy, do you know what I'm going through? That's like saying your overdose never happened."

Sammy looked down. "Most of the time I try to pretend it didn't."

"This isn't something I can just erase."

Sammy stopped walking. "I know, I know. There just doesn't seem like a good answer."

"There isn't," Laura said. She wanted to cry.

"Let me see those pamphlets." Sammy began to flip through them. "These things are so fucking fake. You know, I still have that book you gave me for Christmas, Mary W. Sometimes, I wonder what she would do. Like when I had to confront Jane about leaving me for dead."

"You did that?"

"Yeah, I didn't tell you?

"No."

"Well, I did. And I thought about Mary W. I pictured what she would do if someone played that sick joke on her, and I realized something. She'd fuck them up."

Laura laughed. "So what did you do?"

"I went to Jane's house. Told her if she ever came close to me again, I'd kill her. I had her up against a wall, and I was screaming in her face. Didn't even feel like me." Sammy shook her head. "Must have been all that fear, that anger just raging inside of me. It came out. I think I actually scared her."

"Good."

They were passing small bodegas with yellow signs advertising beer and neon lottery signs flashing in the windows. Clothing stores filled with clothes cheaply made that would tear after a few wears hung on mannequins in odd, suggestive positions. The sun was low over the straight lines of the buildings, vast light rays contrasting with the sharp angles.

Sammy nodded. "I never told you this, but Jane and I were...together."

Laura looked down, silent.

"Laura?" Sammy stopped and tried to catch her eye.

"Why didn't you tell me?"

*Of course, I knew, everyone knew, but why not tell your best friend?*

"I didn't know how to say it. At first, I really liked her. She kind of drew me in. I mean, I've always known I liked girls. I never told you that, I know. But, Jane was my first girlfriend. And, at first, it seemed perfect. Until it really wasn't." Sammy shivered and laughed nervously.

"I guess I kind of knew, without really knowing, if that makes sense. I heard things... rumors. You could've told me."

"It was hard to even figure out what it was myself. Guess we both like to hide."

"Yep, we sure do. And, no, that relationship was seriously not perfect," Laura said, laughing.

"Wow, we've been through some fucked up shit this year," Sammy said. "I love you, Laura."

"I love you too, Sammy." They clasped hands and walked together, perfectly in step.


On Thursday after school, Laura gave Joey another excuse as to why she couldn't come back to his house.

"Just drop me off at Sammy's rehab," she said.

"Does Sammy have rehab on Thursday?" Joey asked.

"I think so. She's been having a tough time. I like to see her afterward for moral support," Laura lied.

"Okay. Well, let me know if you want me to pick you up after."

"No, I'll just walk home."

"Okay."

The car pulled up in front of the brick building that housed both the rehab facility and the clinic. Laura gave Joey a quick kiss and got out of the car.

"I'll call you tomorrow."

Laura waited until Joey sped off and was out of sight to enter the double glass doors leading into the clinic. This time, Ms. Foster was waiting for her in the waiting room. She was smiling and her hands were folded.

"Laura, it's nice to see you. I'm so glad you're back."

"Hi, Ms. Foster," Laura said.

Ms. Foster opened the door for Laura. "Come into my office," she said. "There's someone here I'd like you to meet."

They walked back through the hallway with old green carpeting and bulletin boards filled with pamphlets pinned to the cork. Ms. Foster opened her office door and motioned for Laura to come in and sit. In the other chair, a quiet looking woman who looked to be about fifty sat primly. Her gray hair was trimmed and neat, and there was a small gold cross around her neck. She wore a royal blue blouse with grey slacks that matched the color of her hair. Sensible black shoes peeked out from the cuffs.

"Laura," Ms. Foster said, "I'd like you to meet Stella Chance."

Stella looked at Laura warmly, and there was something in her eyes that reminded Laura of her mother, a sort of understanding or wisdom that she hadn't seen in anyone else before. She shook her hand.

"Stella is a social worker for Catholic Family Services."

"I'm not religious," Laura said quickly. "I mean, my Nana is, but I'm really not."

"That's okay, Laura," Stella said, and her voice poured out like warm honey. "You don't have to be. The organization I work for just wants to help you in whatever way we can."

Laura nodded.

"Catholic Family Services helps young, pregnant women make choices for their babies," Ms. Foster said. " Adoption is one of the options you might want to consider more. Ms. Chance just happened to be here today for a meeting, and I thought she could give you some information that might help you make a decision."

"Call me Stella," she said, smiling.

"Laura," Stella continued. She looked right into Laura's eyes with a penetrating stare that was also kind. "What do you want for your life?"

"What do I want for my life?"

*What kind of question is that?*

"Yes. If you could do or be anything, who would you be?"

"Um. I love music. I like plays and theater."

*What is she getting at?*

"That's wonderful. You could be a musician. Or star in the school play next year. Or go to art school. I want you to have the best chance at a life that you love. And, I also want your baby to have the best possible chance at life too. Adoption is not complex, but it is very deep, and it helps both the mother and the child find an environment where they can thrive."

"I get it, and I've thought about adoption. But how do I just say goodbye and never see it again?"

At this, Stella paused and looked into Laura's eyes again. "It's the hardest thing you will ever do. And, it's the most important thing you can ever do. You are both getting a second chance."

*A second chance. Maddy used to cry long into the darkness. So many diaper changes and unending feedings. Maddy had also clung to Mom she loved and needed her above everything. If I give up the baby, would anyone ever love and need me like that?*

That love, even with the price, was intoxicating.

"I'll think about it some more," Laura said.

Stella nodded at Ms. Foster. "This is Ms. Chance's card, dear. When you make a decision, you can call her."

"One more thing," Stella asked. "Are you getting sufficient care?"

"I haven't been to the doctor at all. I just took a pregnancy test a few weeks ago."

"No matter what your decision, I want you to get the proper care. Here's the address and telephone number for a doctor I recommend. Give her a call, tell her the situation. She'll see you, no problem."

"Thank you," Laura said. She stood to rise. "Goodbye."

"I'll talk to you soon, my dear," Stella said, her eyes reflecting the deep blue of her blouse. They appeared like two oceans to Laura, oceans that might offer a passage to a new chance at life and, at the same time, the worst pain she'd ever have to face.

# March 2001

The bathroom was cold and the tile felt icy beneath Laura's feet as she stepped out of the shower. Her father had made them keep the heat low all winter, and the March sun wasn't strong enough to warm the house. Laura shivered a little bit as she stood in front of the mirror examining her body.

Before meeting Stella, the idea of a baby actually living inside of her had felt nebulous. It was kind of like that disorienting feeling of waking up and not knowing exactly where you were. That happened sometimes at Joey's house, or when she was a little girl and her mother would carry her from her warm bed into her own room. Laura would blink and look around sleepily, trying to place the window position and the smell of the sheets before recognizing it as her own bedroom and drifting back off to sleep.

Pregnancy had been a bit like that, like a spinning top that never fell. Now, it felt stark and real. The spinning had stopped.

Standing in front of the mirror, her nipples had darkened and there was a gentle curve to her belly that had been smooth and flat just a few weeks before. Sometimes, morning sickness lasted all day, and other times Laura felt so tired that she could barely remember her own name.

*Today is an okay day, though.*

She touched her belly and imagined looking inside, peering beneath the layers of tissue, fat, and muscle. The cells of the new life within her replicating like blooming flowers, petals spreading, shedding, growing anew. A formation of something from nothing.

Laura wrapped herself in a towel and walked to her bedroom. The house was quiet, still fast asleep. Her father was home and not home. He had slipped further away ever since that night with Joey. Now, when Laura made a mistake with her careful timing and they did run into each other, he just stared through her with hollow eyes. His face was drawn and black circles shadowed his eyes. Laura began to wonder if he had strayed from solely using alcohol to something harder and even more poisonous, but there was no way to find out for sure, and she didn't want to snoop through his room. She didn't really care, and instead turned ever more inward.

Maddy was sound asleep, her pillow covering one side of her head. Laura tiptoed quietly into the bedroom. Sitting in the drawer of her nightstand, tucked inside of a book, was the card Stella Chance had given her.

*What do I want for my life? I guess I want to get married someday. To Joey? Maybe go to college. Have a job I like, maybe in music or the arts.*

She touched her belly again. *What does this baby want?*

"Certainly not to be born into a shithole like this," Laura muttered a little too loudly and Maddy jerked a little.

Later that afternoon, when Maddy was still at school and Nana was out shopping and her father was at work, Laura picked up the card again and dialed the number on it. The phone rang several times before a chirping voice answered.

"Catholic Family Services, Stella Chance's office, how may I help you?"

"Hi, may I please speak with Ms. Chance?"

"Of course, may I ask is calling?"

"Laura Thompson."

"She'll be right with you."

The phone went silent for what seemed like hours before the warm voice on the other end poured through the phone.

"Hello dear, I was hoping to hear back from you," said Stella. "How can I help you?"

"I've been thinking a lot. I think I'd like to go forward with...with the adoption," said Laura.

"That's wonderful news," Stella said this in a singsong voice like Laura had just told her she had gotten an A+ in math. "Did you call the doctor's number I gave you?"

"I did. I have an appointment in two days."

"Good, we'll want to make sure that baby is healthy. Laura, one more question. Does the father know about all of this?"

Laura sighed. "No, I don't know how to tell him."

"You'll have to, dear, he has the right to know. And part of our process is to meet with the father. We need his consent."

"I know," said Laura in a small voice.

*I just have no idea how to tell him.*

"Talk to him. And I'll meet you at the clinic next week so that we can begin the process. Next Thursday at 4?"

"Next Thursday at 4," Laura repeated.

"Take care of yourself, my dear."

"I will."

Laura hung up the phone.

*Tell Joey.*

Thinking about it hurt her brain. Picking up the phone again, she dialed Sammy's number.

The phone rang several times before Sammy picked up.

"Hello?" Sammy said through a mouthful of food.

"Sammy?"

"Hey, Laura. Sorry, I was just eating. What's going on? Are you okay?"

"Yeah, yeah I'm fine."

*No I'm not.*

"So, what's the verdict? That's why you're calling right? Have you made your decision yet?" Sammy asked.

"I think so," said Laura.

"So what's it going to be?"

"I think I'm going to put the baby up for adoption."

Sammy whistled a little. "You are brave, Laura."

"I hope so," she said. "But now the social worker said that I have to tell Joey."

"No shit, did you just realize that?"

"What do I say?

"I mean, he's 50% of the problem here. It's not like this is completely your fault," Sammy said through a mouthful of food. Laura could almost hear the crumbs flying.

"I know, but still."

"Just tell him. Be straightforward, be honest."

"That's really hard."

"Laura, you can't live your life hiding in the shadows, trying to dodge everyone. Someday, you have to step out, be seen."

"But I've gotten really good at living there."

"I know," Sammy laughed a little. "Me too. That's what we do, right? The world hurts us so we step back, stay hidden. Like shadow sisters."

"You make us sound like vampires," Laura laughed.

"Could be worse, I guess," said Sammy.

"Your Mary W. didn't hide in the shadows. She stepped out."

"She was nearly burned at the stake," Sammy said.

"I know, but at least she was heard," Laura said. She paused. "Okay, I'm going to tell him."

"Okay. I'll be here on the other end of all this," said Sammy. The phone clicked as they both hung up.


The doctor's office was small and bare. Laura had to keep checking and double-checking the address, not sure if she was at the right place. There was a nondescript glass door with the number 43 in peeling white letters. She had looked down at the card: Dr. Li, OB-GYN was printed at the top in thick black font then right below the address, 43 West Main Street.

*Guess this is it.*

It was, but just barely. Most doctor's offices had at least some semblance of decoration on the walls or at least some magazines. This office was bare bones, just a few rows of those folding metal chairs and a radio that hummed static in the background. The receptionist had a mouth that looked like it was drawn with a pencil, and she didn't make eye contact when she handed Laura her paperwork.

"We'll call you in a moment," the monotone voice echoed from behind the glass partition.

Laura nodded and then looked back down at the grey carpet and her knotted fingers. There was only one other person in the waiting room, a young woman who looked only a little older than her. She was clutching her jacket around a very round belly as if she were trying to hide the bump that protruded.

*Why try to hide that here? I mean, we're at an OBGYN for a reason.*

Sammy had asked Laura if she wanted her to come along, but Laura had refused.

"You've done so much already, I can go on my own."

Sammy had looked a little hurt, so Laura quickly said, "It's not that I don't want you there, it's just...I don't know. I'm getting an ultrasound today. What if there's something wrong? I don't know what any of this is going to be like. I feel like I just need to process it inside, process it by myself."

Sammy nodded and squeezed Laura's hand.

"I'll let you know how it goes."

*The minutes are just dragging, maybe I should have let her come.*

"Laura Thompson," called a nurse with a friendly voice.

*Maybe someone is actually cheerful in this dismal place.*

The nurse was wearing bright pink scrubs, and she had a pink scrunchie in her graying hair. Laura followed her through the wooden door and into a narrow corridor.

"First door on your left," the nurse said, smiling.

The door closed behind them with a click, and Laura felt her palms begin to drip. Her throat was suddenly very dry, and she wished she had packed a water bottle.

*Aren't pregnant women always thirsty? Maybe that's why they pee so much.*

"So," the nurse said in the same cheerful voice, "You think you're pregnant?"

Laura looked down and nodded.

"I see here in your paperwork that you're about to turn sixteen. Do you know the father?"

Laura nodded again.

"Well, today we're going to take a look at the baby and see how it's growing. Dr. Li will be in shortly with an ultrasound machine."

Laura looked up, startled.

"Don't worry," the nurse said, reading her mind. "It doesn't hurt a bit. Just feels a bit cold and wet. And, you'll get to see your little one." She smiled.

Laura tried to smile back, but the corners of her mouth seemed to be stuck.

"It's not, not mine," she stumbled. "I'm putting the baby up for adoption. I'd rather not see, I don't think."

The nurse paused and her smile dropped for a moment before returning to her face. "I see. Well, we have to look, but you certainly don't have to. If you want to turn away, that's okay by me. Now, I'm going to have you put on this gown. You can undress fully."

"Okay," Laura said in a small voice.

*An ultrasound. That's going to make this thing so real. What am I even doing?*

The door clicked again behind the bright pink nurse and Laura stood to undress.

The room was cold, and a vent in the ceiling blew even colder air. The hairs on Laura's arms stood at attention, and she felt the icy blast across her breasts as she pulled off her shirt and bra. She pulled on the faded blue gown, and then slid down her pants and underwear. Her legs were shaking a little, whether, from nerves or the cold, or both, she wasn't sure. She held them tightly together. There was a gentle knock at the door.

"Come in."

The door opened again with the bright pink nurse and the doctor, who appeared just as stark and bare as her office. She had on grey pants and a grey shirt, and her white coat had a grey tint to it. Her face wasn't unpleasant, however, and she had warm eyes.

"Laura, I'm Dr. Li." Her tone was direct and businesslike, but not harsh.

"Nice to meet you."

"I'm going to ask you a few questions, and then we'll start the ultrasound. First, it looks like you're around 13 weeks along, based on your missed period. Is that right?"

"Yes."

"Nausea?"

"A little."

"Cramping?"

"Not really."

"Any spotting?"

"No."

"Good. Jenny, can you wheel in the ultrasound machine, please?"

"Now just lay back, Laura. I'm going to apply some jelly to your lower abdomen, it's going to feel a bit cold."

The paper crunched beneath her as Laura lay down on the hard bed. Dr. Li's hands were like ice as she abruptly massaged some of the jelly onto Laura's stomach. Laura bit her lip to keep from gasping.

"Okay, Jenny, lights out, here we go."

Laura turned her head away from the machine and stared at the wall. The glow of the ultrasound machine lit up the room, creating faint shadows.

*Just get this over with.*

Laura could feel her heart beating incessantly. The paper under her hands felt damp and cold. Dr. Li moved the ultrasound wand across her belly, stopping every so often and pressing in, almost painfully.

"I think we've almost got it," Dr. Li said. "Ah, there we go."

Suddenly the room erupted in a noise like tiny, galloping hoofbeats. Laura couldn't help but turn her head.

*Is something wrong?*

"What is that?" She asked.

Jenny turned to her and a smile lit up her face. "The best part of my job. That's the sound of your baby's heartbeat."

"Heartbeat?"

"Yes," Dr. Li replied. "When they're so tiny, the heartbeat is extremely fast. Your little one has a nice, healthy, quick heartbeat. You've got a fighter inside of you. Do you want to see?"

Laura squirmed. "I...I don't know." She felt a warm hand on her shoulder.

"Look," Jenny whispered in her ear. Laura didn't know if Dr. Li even heard. Jenny turned the machine toward Laura, and in front of her was a tiny, baby-shaped blob, if babies could look like amoebas with tiny hands and feet. Laura could see the creature swimming and jumping around.

"Wha-what?" she let out a gasp that turned into a deep sob. "It's so...awake, so active."

Dr. Li smiled in the glowing machine light. "Just a hunch, and we'll have to check later, but I think it's a girl. Normally at this stage, with a boy, you see a little more right here," she pointed toward the legs, giggling a little, not at all like a doctor.

"A girl," Jenny whispered, now putting both of her hands on Laura's shoulders, almost cradling her.

"What do you think, Laura?"

"I think she's amazing."


Wearing a loose fitting jacket and sneakers, Laura walked to Joey's house in the early evening. Nana was making Maddy dinner and her father had left for work.

*It's amazing he still has a job.*

Joey had opened the door with a sweet smile. He was wearing an old sweatshirt that always smelled like home. A pain sliced through Laura's heart.

Sitting on Joey's couch, she slid her fingers through the fog on a cold glass of water while he chatted about working at the garage, night classes, and the band. Apparently, Tim wanted to leave the band. He had a new girlfriend, and she was resentful of the practice time.

"Why doesn't she just come to the band practices like I do?" Laura asked. Her voice sounded surprisingly clear even though her head was swimming.

"Yeah, good question. Well, she's nothing like you," Joey said, smiling.

He sat down next to Laura and wrapped his arm around her. Alcohol used to lace his breath, but recently he smelled more like toothpaste and something spicy that Laura couldn't quite place.

"Joey," she said abruptly.

"What's up?"

"I have something to tell you, and it's going to be a huge shock, but I know I just have to say it and get it over with."

*Can I do it? I have to. I think I'm going to have a heart attack.*

"Okay?" Joey's bright face had darkened.

Laura took a deep breath and held it for a moment. "I'm pregnant."

Joey's head dropped into his hands. When he looked up at her, his face was pale and his eyes looked blank and scared. It was the blank look he had when they first met that had seemed to dissolve.

"Laura, Laura, oh my God. What the fuck?" He stood up and pulled his hair back with both hands so that his forehead looked like a bare dome.

*His hair is getting really long. Wow, why am I thinking about that right now? Breathe.*

The light in the room was fading fast. Joey's dark face looked monstrous, cast in shadows, and the whites of his eyes were bulging and illuminated by the street lamps clicking on outside.

"I know," she said quickly. "That's why I'm arranging an adoption. The details are all being worked out."

"An adoption?" He looked at the ground. "Wouldn't an...abortion be easier?"

"Easier? Joey, none of this is easier. I don't have an easy choice."

"No, no, I know. Just...shit." Joey sat down again, but this time he sat across the room on the couch by the window.

"Do I get a say?"

"Yes, of course. I'm working with a social worker. She wants to meet and talk to you."

Joey nodded, still looking down.

"I love you, Laura." He turned and looked at her. "I think you're amazing. But, I don't know if I can handle this."

"I know. But there's nothing for you to handle." Laura could feel panic rising in her voice and she tried to keep her tone even while her heart beat ferociously. "I'm taking care of it. Everything will go back to normal after the baby's born."

"I really don't think it will." Joey looked sad. Laura realized she had never seen him truly sad.

"It will, Joey," she said. "Just come with me to see Stella next Thursday, that's the social worker."

"So, what do we do in the meantime? Will we still be...together?" Joey asked.

"I'd like to be," Laura said in a small voice.

*Please don't leave me because of this.*

"Me too, but I…I need some time to think…some space. I'll come with you to see the social worker, but after that, I don't know, just give me some time."

"Okay," Laura said.

*I don't want to give you time, I want things to go back to how they were.*

"Do you have any questions?" Laura paused, "I did have an appointment, do you want to see the sonogram?"

"Sure, okay," Joey said, but he didn't move from his place on the opposite side of the room.

Laura pulled out a small strip of photos with a tiny white blob from her bag. Tears began to flood her eyes.

"Here," she said. "The baby is healthy. The doctor thinks it's a girl."

Joey held up the picture of the baby to the window. Light filtered through the foggy, white image of the baby, just a blob of cells, more like a fish than a human. It almost seemed to move in the dimness.

"A girl. Wow. God, I wish you had told me sooner." Joey looked out the window at nothing. "Who else knows?"

"Just Sammy right now."

"Your dad is going to kill you, Laura," Joey said.

"I know." Laura tasted fear on her tongue. "Next, I have to tell Nana. She's not going to be happy, but I'm going to tell her the plan, and hopefully, she'll know what to do about Dad."

Joey nodded. "You could always stay here."

"I've spent so much time running, Joey. I have to face this, face him. But, thanks. I don't know what's going to happen next, but I'll figure it out."

"And who's arranging the adoption?" Joey asked.

"A woman named Stella Chance, from Catholic Family Services."

"You're not religious."

"That's what I said," Laura had to laugh a little. "It's pretty ironic, but she's willing to help me arrange an adoption for the baby."

Joey nodded. "It's getting really dark." He stood to switch on the light and then walked across the room. Sitting next to Laura, he turned to her and held her face in his hands. They felt soft and gentle. She nestled her cheek against his palm.

*Please don't hate me.*

"I don't want to lose this," she said. "To lose us. I felt like I was just beginning to emerge somehow."

"I know," he said tenderly. "And I loved that. I'm going to be here for you, whatever you need, but I have to work this out, think about it. I just need some time."

Laura nodded. "I have to get home."

"Do you want me to walk you?" Joey had never asked before, he had always just done it.

Laura looked at him. "No," she said. "I'll make it fine on my own."

"Okay," he replied, opening the door for her. "I'll see you next week. What time is the appointment?"

"4 o'clock"

"I'll be there."

"Okay." Laura walked down the steps of his house, tears biting her eyes as the cold stung her cheeks. A heavy sadness sat on her heart.

*What did I really expect? A declaration of everlasting love? A promise to someday marry me and keep the baby and love it and live happily ever after?*

Those vague hopes had swirled in the back of her mind, but Joey was no knight on a white horse coming to rescue her from this pain.

*He loves me, but really, I'm on my own.*

The loneliness of that felt like bricks in her chest.

# April 2001

It was unseasonably warm for April. The last dregs of gravel studded snow were melting on the side of the road. Class had let out a little early and the students seemed to bounce out the front doors, the first promise of spring in the air. Laura was wearing a large, baggy sweatshirt to hide her growing belly, but even that felt too hot. She rolled up her sleeves and fanned her collar to get some air. Sweat beaded her forehead, but it wasn't just from the heat of the day. Joey's LeBaron had pulled up to the entrance of the school, and for once she wasn't excited to see him.

"Catch you later," Sammy said with a quick, wistful glance before she was whisked away by friends.

Laura saw Jane pass by, but her eyes were cast down, and she was on the outskirts of the group that surrounded Sammy.

*Good, stay away.*

Laura opened Joey's car door and stepped in, fanning herself from the heat. The old LeBaron didn't have air conditioning, and Joey was lucky if he could get the heat to work in the winter.

"Hey," said Joey. He looked a little brighter.

*That's good.*

"Hey," said Laura. Joey didn't kiss her, but he did place his warm hand on hers. It felt good, despite her own warmth.

"How was school?" he asked.

"Fine. You're so lucky you dropped out. I'm thinking I should do the same."

"You'll be sixteen in a month. But you should stay, it's better. Besides, after the baby's born, you'll want to get a job eventually."

Laura sighed. "I know, but I cannot even imagine going to school with a pregnant belly." The thought made her want to vomit. "It was bad enough going back after my mom died. Now I'm going to go in every day looking like a giant whale, having everyone know what happened? No way."

"So what are you going to do?"

"Probably drop out for the rest of the year. Maybe longer. At least until the rumors die down. I don't want to be there for that."

"Well, I don't blame you."

Joey's car wound through the bustling streets. It seemed that everyone had decided to emerge from hibernation on this day.

"Take a left up ahead. You'll see the big stone church. Her office is attached to that."

"I see it."

The church loomed ahead like a great monument. Laura had always hated going as a child.

*It smelled funny and I always had to dress up. Plus, another world run by men.*

*"Mom, can I be a priest when I grow up?"*

*"Well, not in our family's religion, Laura. I know we only go to church out of respect for Nana, but they have their rules."*

*"Like what?"*

*"Oh, all sorts of things. Things they'll teach you in your religion classes, things they won't. If I had a little more say, we wouldn't ever go again. There's a lot of things they teach that I don't agree with. That I don't want you learning."*

*"Like what?"*

*"Well, take for example what you just said. We have to follow the rules. So many rules at church!" There was a glint of mischief in her mother's eyes.*

*"Isn't it important to follow the rules?" asked Laura.*

*"Sometimes, yes. But not all the time. Sometimes, you have to look inside yourself and ask, is that my rule? Is that really true? For me?"*

*"Like how I can't be a priest. But why?"*

*"The church doesn't let women become priests."*

*"Well that's stupid," Laura said, crossing her arms against her chest.*

*Her mother laughed. "I agree. See, that's one of the silly rules that doesn't make sense to me."*

*"When I grow up, I'm going to start my own church where anyone can be a priest."*

*"I like that idea," her mother said, enfolding her in her arms.*

*Laura buried her head into her mother's shoulder. "Me too."*

Joey pulled the car into the parking lot. It bumped a little on the way in, and Laura's belly lurched.

"Here we are," Joey said. He got out of the car and stood for a moment with his hands in his pockets, looking up at the church.

"Oh, let me get the door for you." Joey ran over to the passenger side and opened the door for Laura.

"Thanks," she said. "I guess we can go in here." Laura pointed at a pair of large wooden doors.

They walked together, side by side, not touching.

"I think this is it," Laura said. "She said on the phone that she'll be expecting us."

Laura pushed the doors open and Joey followed. She quickly scanned the directory posted on the wall with painted black letters, some fading.

**Stella Chance, Social Worker, Room 201** was written toward the bottom.

"This way," Laura said, following the arrows posted next to the sign.

The hallway smelled of incense and paper. Warm air floated in through open windows on one side of the hallway, and muffled chatter snuck through the cracks in the office doors on the other side. Stella's office was all the way at the end. As they reached her doorway, Joey placed his hand on Laura's back for a brief moment.

Stella seemed busy with a stack of papers piled on her desk. Framed photos lined the shelves on the walls--small children posed with Christmas boxes, smiling forced smiles. A pair of women who looked alike, both with long blonde hair and the same smile as Stella. Laura liked seeing the pictures of her family. It made her more real, somehow. Sometimes Stella seemed like a figment, a fairy godmother of sorts, who appeared only when Laura needed her. It was nice to know that Stella had her own life. Laura hoped she was happy.

"Ah, hello both of you. Joey? Nice to meet you." Stella stood and shook Joey's hand warmly. "Have a seat, please. Joey, let me get you another chair." She disappeared for a moment.

"Here you go. Chamomile tea, anyone?"

"I'll take some," said Laura. Joey looked at her like she was crazy.

"What?"

"It's kind of hot for tea."

Stella laughed a little. "It'll be good for her. I'll put extra honey in it." She paused. "Joey, are you sure you don't want any?"

"Maybe next time," he replied.

Stella returned with a large steaming mug and handed it to Laura. She sat down in her chair and folded her hands.

"So, down to business. Joey, Laura has told you everything we've discussed, I assume?"

Joey shifted a little uncomfortably. "Yeah, I think so."

"I know that you're probably still in shock and overwhelmed. What are you thinking right now?" Stella asked. She peered over her glasses at him in a way that was not unkind but scrutinizing.

Joey shifted again. "I told Laura this but...I need some more time to think. I don't know a lot about adoption, how it's going to affect me. I mean, hell, now I'm going to have my kid in some stranger's house. I'll never know them. It's just, it's just a lot." His face was growing flushed and he bounced his knee quickly.

Stella nodded. "All normal feelings, yes. We expect that you'll have questions and thoughts like that. That's why it's so important that you join us for at least one session. Maybe more. Let's see how today goes."

Laura kneaded her hands together like dough. "Can I say something?"

Stella turned to Laura. "Of course, my dear."

"Joey, adoption feels to me simpler, cleaner, almost."

"How?" Joey asked.

"I guess, I think of it as I can have the baby, and a family who can't have children will raise her. But she'll still be mine, ours I mean. It feels like a death. Like my mom. I can't have her here with me, but she's still my mom."

Joey nodded.

*I don't know if he gets it, but I had to say it.*

"Adoption, when it's done well, can be good for both the birth parents and the adoptive parents," Stella said.

Joey made a small noise that sounded strangled. "Okay, but what about the kid? What about her?"

Stella looked at him with her penetrating stare.

"We can't know what she'll think and feel as she grows. I always recommend parents begin telling their adopted children as early as possible so that it is never a shock once they're grown. Some adopted children have trauma, yes. Some don't seem to. That is something the adoptive parents must learn how to work with so that their child grows up happy and healthy."

"Will I get to meet her?"

"If you want to, yes. When Laura gives birth, she will have a small amount of time with the child. I'm going to make sure of it. You can certainly visit and meet the baby. Some fathers like to, some find it difficult."

"This is a lot to take in," Joey said. He shook his head a little bit as if trying to clear it.

"It is, and that's why we're here," Stella said, smiling kindly.


Later, Joey drove Laura home back through the city. The sun still set early, but there were whoops and hollers from the playground and basketball courts. People were out and about, enjoying the lingering warmth of the day.

"I saw snow in the forecast for tomorrow," said Joey.

"No way," said Laura. "It's too warm today."

"Things change."

"They sure do."

The windows were down and a warm breeze blew against Laura's face. *I'm exhausted, that was too much.*

"Do you want to talk about everything?" Joey asked.

"Not now. I've got to figure out how to tell Nana and eventually Dad."

Joey sighed. "I know. Hey, I still need some time to process this, and I can't just jump back to where we were. But I get the stuff with your dad, and if you need me, I'm here."

Laura nodded. "Thanks."

When they reached Laura's door, Joey hugged her tightly but he didn't kiss her like he normally did.

*Will he ever? I think so, but how can I know for sure? I guess I can't worry about it now. Other things to focus on, bigger issues.*

"I'll call you tomorrow, okay?"

Laura opened the car door.

"Okay," she said.

The lights in the duplex were low even though the sun was setting. There was a faint smell of food, but it might have been the neighbors cooking.

*Not sure if anyone is home.*

She shut the car door, a fog around her head.

The front door was slightly ajar.

"Hello? Anyone home?"

*What happened? Did somebody break in?*

Laura's heart was in her mouth.

"Nana? Maddy? Dad?"

*Please don't be home, Dad.*

There was a rustling sound coming from the back of the duplex. It sounded like it was coming from her bedroom.

"Hello?" Laura called again. The rustling was growing louder. Now there were banging sounds, too.

Laura's body grew cold. Her bedroom door was wide open and her father was in there. Garbage bags surrounded him with Laura's clothes pouring out. There were books in another bag. Her box filled with her mother's things and mementos from her babyhood were spilled across the room. The world turned upside down. Fear left Laura's body, but it was replaced by rage.

"Dad," she screamed. "What are you doing?"

He turned, wobbling a little on his feet. Somehow, he seemed surprised.

*Didn't he hear me calling? He's raving drunk again.*

"What am I doing?" He yelled. "What am I doing?"

He stood over her like a great giant, towering. Laura looked up at him. His mass had always seemed so intimidating, but ever since that night when Joey came to dinner, her father seemed like a small man hiding behind a giant facade.

*Like the Wizard of Oz, a small, scared man behind a curtain. I know he could hurt me if he wanted to. He's strong. I'm stronger.*

Laura took a breath. "Dad, what's going on?"

Her father held a small white card in his hand. It looked like a toy flag, waving in an invisible wind, flickering back and forth.

*What is that? Oh shit. It's Stella's card.*

*Catholic Family Services.*

*Adoption.*

*Written right on the front.*

His voice dropped to a hissing, slightly slurred, whisper. "This...this is what's going on. Did you think you could hide this from me?"

His eyes seemed to roll back in his head and a blue vein throbbed at his temple. The smell of whiskey was strong. Disgust ran through Laura as she imagined him touching all of her things.

Laura was silent. Words were forming in her mind then evaporating. All she could do was stare straight ahead.

"Nothing to say?" He was closer now, too close. Her chin throbbed with the memory of his hands grabbing her face, twisting her neck. "Didn't I always tell you? You're a slut. A good for nothing whore, and now this proves it."

"Dad, I'm taking care of everything. That's why I have the card, that's why I went to see her, the social worker." The words squeaked out. Her father didn't seem to hear anything she said.

"Your mother was a whore and now look at you, following in her footsteps. You must feel so proud."

"Don't talk about my mother."

"What?" Her father squinted his eyes. The look was monstrous.

"I said, don't talk about Mom like that." Laura's voice was louder, stronger.

"Listen, you little bitch, I'll talk about anyone anyway I choose."

His body loomed directly over Laura now. A giant crow with outstretched wings, his mouth a beak ready to bite. The heat from his body emanated outward, suffocating her. His hands wrapped around the neck of her sweatshirt and he pressed her up against her bedroom wall.

"Don't!" She yelled.

"What are you afraid of?" Her father said laughing maniacally. The pressure around her neck was growing more intense. Laura felt the choking sensation travel down into her belly.

*The baby.*

"Jacob!" The voice was sharp and quick. Laura's father, caught by surprise, dropped her and Laura fell to the ground, rubbing her throat and coughing.

"Maddy, call 9-1-1." Laura heard thumping footsteps as Maddy ran to the kitchen for the phone.

Her father swayed a bit and then crumpled to the ground. He folded into himself, rubbing his forehead and moaning. Then he suddenly looked up and roared at Nana, "She's pregnant, you know. I told you, I told all of you."

Nana whipped around to look at Laura. "Is this true?"

Laura nodded. Nana's eyes flashed. "Come with me. Gather your things."

Sirens began to blare, sharp and clear.

The next hour was a blur.

*Police.*

*Paperwork.*

*Handcuffs.*

*Dad's eyes were red and raw looking at me from the back of the police car.*

*I'm all right.*

*No really, I'm okay.*

*I don't need to go to the hospital.*

*Nana.*

*A car ride, Maddy next to me.*

*Leaving another home.*

*My stuff in the trunk.*

*Where to now?*

Nana's car pulled up to her old apartment.

"You can stay here for the time being. Your father was arrested, but I don't know how long they'll hold him or what will happen next." Nana, always shrinking against her son, seemed to have suddenly bloomed as well.

They walked inside, Laura still in a daze. The apartment smelled a little musty like the windows hadn't been opened in months.

*They probably haven't been.*

Nana had a tenant, but they left a while back, and she was never able to fill the vacancy. She fussed around the apartment, wiping everything with paper towels and making up the bed with old sheets from the linen closet. Maddy sat with Laura on the loveseat.

"It's true, Laura? You're having a baby?"

"Oh, you heard Dad yell that? Yeah," Laura sighed. "I can't hide it anymore, obviously."

Maddy moved a little closer to Laura. She put her arm around her and snuggled her small head against her shoulder.

"Thanks, Maddy," Laura said.

Nana emerged from the bedroom. The steely look was still in her eye.

"Laura, I'll head back to the duplex with Maddy for the time being to arrange everything for your father. I expect he'll be heading back to rehab, but I can't be sure, and you'll be safe here, especially in your...condition. You said you're taking care of everything?"

Laura nodded. "I've decided to put the baby up for adoption, and I'm working with a social worker."

"Good. I'll check on you, and if you need anything, you know where to call. Best to stay here for now, yes," Nana said, almost to herself. "Okay, say your goodbyes for now girls. We have a road ahead of us, that's for certain."

# May-June 2001

The Earth turned over and yawned awake. Laura, too, was living in a liminal world, somewhere between winter and summer. Her belly, a glowing sun, grew brighter each day, as her axis turned and reached toward the light. Her breasts sat roundly on the dome of her abdomen, and in the evenings, she rested a mug of hot chocolate there.

During the day, Laura moved slowly, heaving her girth around the small apartment. It smelled like Nana's rose perfume, and there were pictures everywhere.

*Why do old people like to decorate their houses with pictures? I guess, by a certain age, that's all they have left. The ties, the connections to a younger life filled with children and noise, have died off. Maybe it's a replacement for the quiet that happens when those children grow up and leave.*

Laura spent many hours walking through the rooms, tracing the faces with her fingertips. She especially loved the pictures of her mother when she was young. Laura would use her pinky finger to erase her father from the picture and sit and gaze into her mother's eyes. She looked bright and happy.

In one, her mother was sitting under a willow tree with a sunhat that covered one eye, so that she appeared to be winking. A picnic blanket was spread on the grass, and she was holding an apple in one hand. It had a bite out of it. Laura loved this photo most. It had action, personality, rhythm. Her mother had just bitten the apple, she could probably still taste its sweet juice on her lips as she smiled for the photo. The smile was genuine, and a little sneaky, like she was planning something.

On the other side of the camera sat her father, young, happy, not swept away from himself by alcohol and self-hatred. Laura liked to think that somewhere these people existed. They still sat beneath this tree, in love, with all of the hope in the world available to them.

Laura had slunk out of school in April, swiftly filling out all of the necessary forms and paperwork and then slid out of the big red double doors, letting them bang shut with a satisfying slam behind her. She was sixteen. It was legal, and she couldn't stand letting anyone see her belly grow.

Very few people had crossed her path in the last two months. Nana stopped by with Maddy every few days for a visit. At night, Sammy would come over. She often stayed with Laura, keeping her company.

Nights were the hardest.

The baby would dance, pressing into Laura's lungs and hipbones, and Laura would lie awake staring at the moonlight on the ceiling. Sammy slept next to her in the large bed, her regular breathing soothing Laura despite her insomnia. Sometimes, they would intertwine fingers and Laura could feel the steadiness of Sammy's grip. She needed that.

Joey stopped by after work occasionally, but everything between them felt stilted and awkward. Laura missed the blossoming days, when they were discovering each other. That time felt like a song she had once known and had now forgotten the words to, but it held a note of sweetness that she carried with her. Laura didn't feel angry at Joey.

*I don't really expect that much of the people around me anymore.*

A year ago, this realization would have angered her immensely. Now, sitting with a big, round belly in an old woman's apartment, surrounded by ghosts, Laura was keenly aware that nothing lasts. There was a sort of peace in that.

By the summer solstice, her stomach had grown to a full moon and everything beneath it had disappeared. In quiet moments she began to say goodbye to the life that was still growing inside of her. The baby, moving, kicking, breathing, squirming, sleeping, eating, didn't belong to her, but to a life that was not her own. It was odd to be so close to something and know, at the same time, that soon it would be gone forever.

Stella had begun to prepare her for that goodbye. They met weekly. Laura would take the bus there on Wednesdays, wearing a giant, baggy sweatshirt that made her so hot her skin itched, but she preferred that to the stares.

Stella's office sitting in the church hall was a reminder. It reminded her of Nana's devoutness that wasn't enough to save her. Of her mother's funeral. There was always a smell of dried flowers and stale coffee. There was lots of paperwork and forms to fill out. They wanted to make sure she was in her right mind in agreeing to give up her baby. Joey attended a few more of the meetings, too. He was there, but not there.

*He just wants to get this over with, I can tell. I think he's made some sort of peace with the goodbye, and now he's impatient and twitchy during the meetings.*

Laura has six weeks to change her mind once the child is placed for adoption, but she knew that she wouldn't do that, to herself, to the family. She'd had enough loss in her life to know how devastating it would be to inflict that on someone else.

*It would be like murder.*

On an especially hot day, a few weeks before her due date, Laura carried the weight of her belly on and off the bus for a final visit with Stella. For the next few weeks, she was asked to rest and only leave the house for doctor's visits. Nana agreed to stop by a few times in the coming weeks with groceries. Sammy said she would clean the apartment. Laura was sinking into a hole and, despite the bright sunshine, the world was freezing over in preparation for her quiet hibernation.

The bus inched through the sweltering streets like an earthworm. Laura could feel every bump and hiccup in her bones. A few people stared at her. Even with her giant sweatshirt, her bump could be seen resting on her lap. Finally, the bus lurched to a stop in front of the large stone church, and Laura rose slowly, holding onto the handrails for support. She squeezed by the people standing, feeling the stares like daggers driving into her body. A few men stepped aside for her and one smiled kindly, but Laura was too self-conscious to acknowledge him.

*God, don't look at me.*

She took the stairs carefully, and then stepped into the hot sun, relieved to have been spit out of the sweating, heaving animal.

Stella was waiting in her office, working quietly at her desk, stacks of papers surrounding her tiny frame so that she was nearly hidden, swallowed by her own responsibility. When Laura walked in, flushed and out of breath, Stella didn't even hear her.

"Stella?" Laura said hesitantly. Stella looked so serious.

*I don't want to interrupt her.*

Stella's head whipped upward and she lowered her glasses. "Hello, my dear. I didn't even hear you come in. Come, sit down. You must be exhausted. Take off your sweatshirt, we all know what you're hiding under there," she said laughing.

Laura smiled. Stella rose and walked out of the room for a moment. She always made her a cup of chamomile tea with honey, and no matter how hot she was from the bus ride, Laura always accepted.

"Put your feet up, dear," Stella said, pulling a chair next to Laura's so she could raise up her puffy ankles. "There you go."

Stella sat down in a small armchair across from Laura.

"Now. It's our last session here. The next time I see you, you'll be in the hospital. I'll be there to help the process of giving the baby over to the foster home where she'll stay while the prospective parents finish the approval process." Stella paused. "How are you doing?"

Laura shrugged. "Sometimes it feels real and scary, and sometimes it doesn't."

"That's normal," Stella replied, nodding. She moved a piece of gray hair out of her face. "You're going to love your child, that's natural, but in a different way than other mothers do. From afar, as a memory."

"A ghost."

"Yes," Stella said. "A ghost. But only a ghost to you. She will go on to grow up and have a wonderful life with wonderful people, we will make sure of that."

"But, she won't know me."

"Not unless she searches for you. Her file won't be given to her until she's eighteen."

"Eighteen. I'll be thirty-four years old by then. A real grown-up," Laura said. She looked out the window. The bus was making another round. "I wonder what she'll look like."

"You'll be able to hold her, to look into her eyes and memorize her face on the day she's born. You may keep a baby photo if you'd like."

*To put with all the other ghosts in Nana's apartment.*

She looked down.

"We have a few more papers to fill out. Normally, I save these for the end. They are the most...personal." Stella handed Laura some forms with large blank boxes across them.

"You'll be writing a little bit about yourself, anything you'd like the family and the child to know about you."

Laura looked down at the page. The boxes looked enormous.

*Where do I even start?*

Stella seemed to sense her frustration.

"Don't think too hard about it, just a few simple things. It will be a way for the parents to place some of the child's talents or challenges, their appearance. We think of it as an anchor to their origin."

Laura nodded. She picked up her pen to write. Interests. Playing the guitar and writing. Appearance. Tall, thin, long brown hair, straight as a pin. Her hair never could hold a curl.

*I feel like I'm trying to take my whole life and shrink it down to a few bullet points, digestible to a family that will never truly know me. I'm going to be remembered by this child as just a few sentences.*

Laura looked up from the form.

"What's the matter, dear?" Stella peered at her over her glasses behind the stack of paperwork she had gone back to while Laura was finishing her own.

"These sentences, it all just seems so...trivial. So pointless. There is so much more about me she won't know. I wish I could tell her somehow."

Stella stood up and walked across the small room and stood in front of Laura. She bent down and placed her hands, blue with veins and crinkled like a folded fan, on top of Laura's.

Looking her straight in the eye with a gaze that was as hard as steel and as soft as a warm sweater she said, "Then write. Write letters to your baby. You can't send them to her now, but maybe someday you will. Or at least you'll let yourself be seen. Even if it's just by you."

Later that evening, as the sun turned the sky a dusky gray dappled with orange, Laura sat in front of an open window in the bedroom at Nana's writing desk. The sultry breeze tousled her hair. In front of her was a marble notebook she had found in a drawer in the kitchen. A few notes and grocery lists had been written in the front pages by Nana, but other than that it was blank. She stared out the window for a moment, listening to the sounds of cars and the noises of life happen below her. The baby kicked. Laura picked up a pen and began to write.

# Composition Book

Letters to

Elizabeth

June 20, 2001

Dear Elizabeth,

This is my first letter to you, but it won't be my last. I'm not sure where to begin, but I guess I'll just start. My name is Laura Thompson, and I'm your mother. That feels really weird to write.

A mother?

It's true, I suppose, but when I think of "mother" I think of my mom. Moms wake up at night to tuck you back in, they kiss booboos and make cookies.

Right?

My mom did those things. My mom kept me safe from, well, everything. Am I your mother?

Somewhere, in a file tucked far away, you'll find my name and you'll see I really am your mother. But I'm not your mom. I'm not going to be there for all those little moments, so even though you live inside of me now, you will be loved and cherished (I hope) by some other lady.

What I'm trying to say is even though I'm not your mom, I'll always be your mother. Please don't forget that. But maybe it's easier if I just call myself Laura for now.


Love, Laura

July 1, 2001

Dear Elizabeth,

I wish you could know me, like really know me, but then I wonder, do we ever actually know our parents? I don't. Mom (your grandma) hid herself, even from me. To me she was love, to others she was perfect. To Dad, she was some sort of victim of his own fears and addiction. But who was she in the quiet moments? In her tiny pockets of peace? That I'll never know. Just like you'll never know that about me.

Maybe when your new parents talk about me they'll feel jealous. Jealous that I got to know you now. Jealous that you're not truly theirs. Or maybe they'll be really cool and just say the truth.

She loved you.

Not that they'll know that for sure. They'll just know the paperwork. But I'm saying it here.

I loved you. I love you.

Maybe with a parent that's the only real thing you need to know. The other stuff is just human bullshit.

My social worker, Stella, told me adoption is like giving you wings and letting you fly. I get that. I'm setting you free. In doing that, though, I have to lock myself away. A part of me that will always remember will live in me forever. But I can't let that be everything, can I? I mean, I can't walk down the aisle to my future husband with you attached to my mind, right? I can't go back to school with the ghost of a baby attached to my hip.

I have to let the prison be okay. But how?

Love, Laura

September 2, 2001

Dear Elizabeth,

It took me a while to be able to write this, but Stella thought it might help to start writing again.

I miss you.

I love you even though I barely knew you.

I named you Elizabeth, even though that will never be your real name. They told me that your adoptive parents are going to keep it as your middle name. You looked like an Elizabeth to me. I'm not sure what an Elizabeth looks like, actually, but if I were to guess, it would be you. Elizabeth makes me think of princesses and castles, knights slaying dragons, and saving the day. I hope that you grow up to be a princess, sweet Elizabeth. I hope you hold that name close to your heart and maybe sometimes, you'll think of me.

I filled out all those forms--height, hair color, eye color, interests. That's just a photocopy of me, it's not the real thing. Stella suggested I write these letters. I'm not going to send them. I wouldn't even if I could. Separation, that's the important thing, Stella said. Too confusing for you to know me. But that's okay. I'll tell you everything here, and maybe someday when you're grown, you'll know me and I'll know you.

Anyway, Elizabeth. I thought that was a pretty name. You were so pretty. I had no idea what giving birth would be like. That definitely scared me. I called Nana (she's your great-grandma) when my water broke. I had just gotten out of the shower and was standing in the bathroom in Nana's apartment and, all of a sudden, a flood. I thought I peed my pants! Not that I was wearing pants at the time, thank goodness, or they would have been soaked. Nana came over quickly with Maddy. I told them not to rush. The doctor said first labors take a while, maybe even a full day. When I heard that, I was scared. A whole day in labor? But you were kind to me. Within a few hours, the contractions started and we went to the hospital. Oh, and I called Sammy and Joey before we left. Maddy had to wait in the waiting room at the hospital, but Nana was in the room with me the whole time.

Everything went so perfectly, little girl.

The contractions hurt, oh boy did they hurt. The nurse, she was young, probably only five or six years older than me, and she held my hand. Made me do this breathing thing. I guess it helped. Then the pain meds came. Now that helped. I think I fell asleep a few times, I could barely feel the contractions. Nana stuck by me though. She held my hand, too.

The young nurse, Sara was her name, played some music on the radio. I think I forgot that we were going to say goodbye. Maybe it was the drugs. Sometimes, it seemed like I was floating. I was so focused on my body that at times I forgot about yours. What you were doing. How you were feeling in there. I hope you weren't scared.

The doctor came in after a few hours and told me to push. I did. They said I did a great job. You came out so quickly, too quickly. The young nurse wrapped you in a clean white blanket that smelled like hospital soap. Stella came and Nana got Maddy from the waiting room. Sammy wasn't allowed in. She said that was okay, she wanted to be there for moral support anyway, even from afar. We each held you. Stella fought for that. She warned me that many birth mothers don't get to hold their babies. They're taken right away. But I got to hold you. I am so happy about that.

Maybe they think it makes the goodbye harder, but I don't know. I'm glad I have that memory, even if it's hard sometimes. Well, a lot of the time.

Your daddy held you too. His name is Joey. We looked at you and tried to decide who you looked like. I said you looked like me. He thought you looked like him. Maybe we're both right. I definitely saw his nose and his chin. But your eyes. Your eyes are mine. Bright blue, and fair skin like me. We think you have red hair, but it was hard to tell. When the nurse, Sara, washed you, there was a pale orange glow on the top of your head. That would be so pretty. A princess named Elizabeth with red hair.

They took you away not long after.

That's the part I still have nightmares about.

I didn't know what it was like to love a baby. I'm not even sure if I loved you when you were inside of me. You felt more like a part of me, and I was having trouble loving myself. But when I saw you, I loved you. I knew you were real. A person with a beating heart and lungs. Two eyes, ears that could hear, a mouth that could taste, talk and cry. You barely cried you know. I held you against me. My breasts ached. Stella had warned me about that, too. I wanted to nurse you so much, but I couldn't. But when I held you there, you fell fast asleep. It was so beautiful to watch.

It's hard to remember the goodbye, it's blurry, like trying to look through a foggy window. There are shapes and colors, but no definition. I wake up in the night shaking a lot.

A dream keeps visiting me: a doctor with Dad's face, mouth wide open, jaws lined with sharp wolf teeth, pulling you out of my arms, me screaming. I hate that dream. It's so hard to move forward with that dream haunting me.

But I'm trying. Believe me I am.

Stella gave me your little picture. I put it in the corner of the picture frame with Mom. I think you two would have liked each other. My two ghosts living somewhere in the past, somewhere in

time where I cannot reach you. Maybe, in some way, you are together. I hope that for both of you.

Love, Laura

October 1, 2001

Dear Elizabeth,

You're almost three months old right now; I can't believe it.

Time seems to have stretched like a rubber band since I gave birth to you. My body is back to normal, for the most part. When I look in the mirror,  I look less like a pear and more like a square, though.

My mind hasn't gotten back to normal, but I'm feeling better, a little every day. School helps. I decided to go back. Joey helped me make that decision, and I feel pretty good about it. School was never hard for me. Maybe it was too easy, boring at times. But you need it, they say, to do things like getting a good job. I guess I don't want to flounder this chance, this second chance. You got yours, now I need to take mine. Plus, it gives me something to focus on. Something real, not just a figment from the past.

I'm thinking about Mom less, too, and Stella says this is a good thing. At first, I felt really guilty about it, like the memories kept her alive. But I kind of see what Stella's saying. It's true, living in a distant past, half made-up, there's nothing there. No substance.

I'm still living at Nana's place. Maddy comes by after school sometimes. (She's your aunt). She's getting cooler. She loves comic books and we read them together or watch TV. I wish you could get to know her. I like that she doesn't care what anyone thinks. Not friends at school. Not Nana. Definitely not Dad. Dad never turned on her, but she watched all of it.

God, I'm glad that's over.

I haven't talked much about your grandfather. I think, when he was younger, he had a lot of potential. Mom always said he

squandered his talents. He ended up a night shift security guard, and he drank a lot. A few months ago he went to rehab for like the millionth time. It might have actually worked this time, though. We're going to see. He's living back at the duplex where we all used to live together (me, Nana, Dad, and Maddy). Nana said he's been sober, no relapses. He's quiet though. She says he talks about me like someone who's died. I haven't seen him since the day I left and came to live in Nana's apartment. We're supposed to see each other again, but in a therapist's office, in a few weeks.

We'll see how that goes.

If you met him when he was sober and happy, he would be a different person. When he's drunk, he's mean and paranoid and just crazy. I learned not to be afraid of him because he always made me so afraid. It's funny how that happened.

Something else happened a few weeks ago. You'll probably learn about this in school someday. The Twin Towers, these two really tall buildings in New York City, were hit by planes that were hijacked by terrorists. It was really scary and sad. I was sitting in period two math class when an announcement came over the loudspeaker.

"We just received word that one of the Twin Towers has been hit by a plane. We are awaiting more information."

At first, I thought that maybe the pilot had fallen asleep. Kind of like a driver falling asleep at the wheel.

An hour later we had another announcement-it was confirmed terrorism. By then I was in period four English. My teacher, Mrs. Dawson, rolled the old television cart over and tried to plug it in to watch the news, but of course, it didn't have cable. No one knew what was going on. They dismissed us early, and I had to walk home because Joey didn't know that school had let out. That was a long walk. I saw people crying in the streets. There was a television blaring from a cafe so I stepped inside just long enough to watch.

So many people died.

So much pain.

I saw that and of course, I thought of you. Do you really want to be in this world? Are you going to be sorry that I had you, made you live a life in such a God-awful place? When I saw Joey, he was crying.

I've only seen him cry once before, the day we had to say goodbye to you.

But on that day, he left the garage early and came straight to Nana's. Maybe he thought I'd be home or heard schools were getting let out, I don't know. We sat on the couch watching the television, holding hands. Things had been so weird between us since we found out about you, but that day something clicked. Maybe it was everything we'd been through together or seeing all the tragedy for people less than one hundred miles away from us. Something happened, though, and suddenly we were back together, and it was like it used to be.

We watched the grief of everyone we knew pour out like oceans, and suddenly it felt okay to be sad all the time. I think it's also what helped me understand my sadness for you.

It was okay to be sad, to feel sad, to cry. I was grieving for our country, for the world, for myself, for Dad, for Mom, for you. I hope when you someday learn about 9/11 you feel it, not just know it, but feel it. That way everyone who died will be remembered, even by strangers. They'll live on. Just as you do, somewhere inside of me.

Love, Laura

June 29, 2003

Dear Elizabeth,

I know it's been a while since I wrote to you. Right now, you're about to turn two years old somewhere.

Here's something to celebrate: I just graduated from high school!

I can't even believe it myself.

Walking that stage felt like a dream come true. Even with everything that happened, I graduated with honors. Nana and Maddy stood up to cheer as I grabbed the diploma. I held onto it with my life. Dad wasn't there.  He's two years sober, but we still don't have much of a relationship. When I do see him, it's usually in a therapist's office. There is still a lot to talk about, to work on. I will probably never have a real relationship with him, like the kind of father-daughter bond you see on cards in the Hallmark aisle. There's just too much there. Too much pain, too much sadness. I'm happy for him, though. From afar.

Here's something I learned--you can love someone without trusting them with your heart. With that kind of love, it's best to love from far away. I can't risk the hurt again, but I can still love him.

Anyway, graduation was a blast. After the ceremony, we went to the beach and had a huge picnic with some other kids from school. Sammy was there. She has a new girlfriend, Lindsey. She's a lot nicer than Jane, thank God.

You're probably wondering what I'm going to do next with my life. Well, I don't know. I didn't apply to colleges last fall like other kids were doing. I just don't feel ready. Maybe I'll take a year off, find a job, decide what I like. Either way, I'm not sure, and I'm okay with that.

And you are hitting your own milestones!

Sometimes at night I close my eyes and imagine you--a little girl with soft, red curls bouncing around your house. In my mind, you have a warm, cozy bed and two loving parents who read you stories and tuck you in at night. You have a dog, too. And your house is small and full of love, like mine was once upon a time, a long, long time ago. You have all of that in my imagination and that gives me comfort.

At the mall I see little kids with their moms, holding their chubby little hands, and I think of you. The clear ring of your baby laughter, your first step, your first word. I've missed all of it. But I haven't forgotten you. You haven't disappeared. I've just made up a different you in my mind to replace the you, I lost.

It's a happy you, one that I hope with all my heart exists.

Love, Laura

August 20, 2004

Dear Elizabeth,

I think you'd be really proud of me. Maybe you will be, someday. Tomorrow I fly out to California to start my freshman year at UCLA. I'm majoring in musical theater. Joey's really jealous. He said that if I become famous, I'll need to take his band along for the ride. We'll see about that.

Stella helped me apply and get a scholarship. She has been so amazing in my life, opening all the right doors at exactly the right moment. Nana said she was proud of me, and I think she's happy to get her apartment back, finally. She's moving there with Maddy. Dad had another relapse, and he's back in rehab. I'm hoping they caught it early this time before he really spiraled. Nana's hopeful, too. Dad knows I'm going to California, but our therapist decided it would be best not to meet in person. I had a quick phone call with him to let him know.

He said he was proud of me. I couldn't believe it.

I've never heard him speak those words before.

Joey's staying here in Connecticut. He's happy working at the garage. They made him manager a few months ago. I wanted to stay here with him, but he wanted more for me. He helped me realize that I want more for myself. We promised to email and call.

I'm sad and not sad.

I don't want him to become yet another relic of my past, but I have to see what else is out there for me. He's driving me to the airport to say goodbye. Nana and Maddy wanted to come too, but I want that time to be for Joey. They seemed to understand. I think about you all the time, still. We're not that far apart, in age I mean. I'm nineteen years old and you're three. When you think about it, it's not that much time until you're in my shoes.

Time flies, right? Who are you now, I wonder?

Part of me wanted to stay for Joey, but another part of me wanted to stay here for you. You're probably not too far away, somewhere with a family nearby. That's what Stella said, at least.

Local families. Local.

That means that you could be just a few miles away. Did you start preschool yet? I bet you're so smart. Are you good at reading? Maybe not yet, but if you take after me, you will be. Not so much with math though, I never could get the numbers thing down.

I'm leaving tomorrow, but I'm not leaving you. You'll always be with me.

Love, Laura

November 11, 2004

Dear Elizabeth,

I'm writing from my tiny dorm room in California, a sentence three years ago I never could have dreamed of writing. It's midnight here. I got off the phone with Joey an hour ago, he's been having trouble sleeping lately. He thinks about you, too. My roommate is asleep, so I just have my tiny desk lamp on. It's just bright enough to see the page in this journal. I think I'm going to have to get a new notebook soon; I'm almost at the end.

I've been thinking about you, as always. I've been thinking that I can't teach you anything. I miss that. I miss not knowing what that's like. So, I decided to put some things down here, and who knows, maybe someday you'll read them:

- Most people are going to tell you not to feel. Your mom might  tell you to stop crying or your dad might say you need to snap out of it. I'm here to tell you that it's okay if you can't stop crying or snap out of it. That took me a long time to learn. Some feelings will be a tsunami and others will be a short rainfall. Both are okay. When you learn to surf the tsunami and not try to stop its flow, life gets better.

- When you fall in love for the first time, you're going to want to   bend over backwards for the person. You're going to want to meld into them like melting popsicles. It's going to feel amazing but don't. Don't lose yourself to love. It will feel like everything and nothing, and you will find that there is a space in between. That is where you must find the balance. Love will tear you apart and turn you inside out. Let that wash over you, don't let go of your hold on you.

- When I was a kid, I hated being different. It made me sick to my stomach. Now, I kind of like it. In our theater classes, we learn to draw on our experiences, especially our painful ones, to feel our character's emotions. Those hard things are a part of me now, and they have value. I see that. You're going to be different, too. And it's going to be hard. You might want to keep it a secret that you're adopted, but it's going to come out. Friends will ask, you might feel safe and tell someone. Then they'll look at you like you have three heads. Believe me, I know what it's like to feel different. But if there's one thing I've learned, it's this:

We are pushed into the shadows. We are made to feel small and useless and worthless. But it's not the truth. It's not who we are. We are made to shine, Elizabeth. I hope you see that. Come out, sweet girl, and let yourself be seen. Then you will know, the shadows were an illusion all along.

Love, Mom

P.S. This was the last page. Guess I need a new notebook.

# Acknowledgments

Writing this book has been an amazing experience. I want to first thank the dedicated publishing team at Nymeria Publishing, Kennedy Champitto, and Sarah Caro. I appreciate your time, talent, and attention to my novel.

I also want to thank my husband whose support allowed me the time and space to write, even while raising two energetic young children!

I'd like to acknowledge my birth mother, the mother I've never known, but who inspired this story.  I hope this retelling honors you.

I'd also like to thank my mom and dad. Your love and support has made everything possible.

Shannon Marzella is an author and poet. She loves trees, books, and tea. Shannon lives in Connecticut with her husband and two children.